The Future Is Short

The Future Is Short
Science Fiction in a Flash

Editors
Jot Russell
Paula Friedman
Carrol Fix

An Anthology by 32 Authors
With an Introduction by Jot Russell

Lillicat
Publishers
USA

CreateSpace format consultant, Tom Tinney PiR8@conservativebiker.com

Table of Contents

INTRODUCTION

Everything in life is better when shared, but how do you share a dream? How can you capture the intangible nature of imagination?

Write it down.

Within each of us, there is a story just waiting to be told. We are here to tell you that you can write that story, but perhaps not without a little help. The Science Fiction Microstory Contest was created as a method for writers to perceive their words through the eyes of other artists. With little more than a pen, words can be formed into a plot, just as a brush is stroked across the canvas or chords are echoed into a melody. But who's to say the work is actually art?

You be the judge.

These folds of parchment contain but a sampling of stories that have been posted on the contest. Each has undergone the scrutiny of review by the same writers hoping their story will edge past to be the winner. Every month, the vote tallies are collected until one reaches the majority. And under the light of a new moon, the competition starts all over again.

From themes of green or blue, future or past, animal or mineral or alien, a catalyst is formed that sets creativity in motion. By the random nature of synapse, a story forms from thin air, like magic. Bounds that Einstein placed upon light itself cannot hold back a thought. For, imagination is beyond the bars of time and space. Within the mind, and with fewer words than those needed to paint a picture, a full science fiction work is derived in micro-scale.

Which do you like best? Cast your vote!

Jot Russell
Science Fiction Microstories Contest Director

TIME-SLIP

1. Town Line Road

Jot Russell

If you asked, I'd say guilt was my motivator. You see, I built it because I got a man killed once. I was just a careless kid, weaving my green Wolverine bike across the streets, daring cars to hit me. Two had screeched to a halt as I shot across from side roads. I remember stopping there for a giggle, pausing to watch other cars zoom past on Town Line Road before kicking the pedals to life in a path towards destiny.

It took me a few seconds to reach full speed. As I approached the main road, a truck came up fast over the hill and I felt as if I knew I was already dead. When the body lets go of the soul, time suddenly becomes a meaningless thing. Tumbling in the air, suspended in a state of weightlessness, everything I had ever done in my life was relived in a single moment. Six years in the span of a second, until the second passed, and time itself suddenly returned to me.

Oh, how I wish that, when I stood up to cry, it was for him. But the fear of self-preservation took hold of that remaining part of my soul. My thoughts at that moment completely disregarded the single glance that I had made at the ruins of my bike next to the broken form of the man who had jumped out from behind a tree on the sidewalk and threw me from my bike. Now, he's all I can see.

***

As I became a man, I told myself to make the life he saved worth something. But my degree at MIT and research work at Google Labs failed to quench the guilt that I still felt. One thing I can say is that I didn't let it

3

slow me down. Drawing from the accumulated regret, I pushed forward knowing the answer was there; somehow suspended in time and just waiting to be discovered. Forty years after that fateful day, I realized I could build it.

A hundred years before, the simple word "energize" introduced most to the notion of a transporter. But deep within the energy that all matter is created from was the real solution. How could it have been so simple?

Once completed and mass-produced, no one would need a car, truck, or van. A revolutionary solution to so many of society's problems. A clean, quiet and safe world from the likes of tin mechanized bullets that traveled on land and air. The tests were far from perfect, but each failure only extended my understanding of the science and increased my resolve to make my dream a reality. And then it was!

Through quantum's uncertainty between time and space lay a dimensionless shortcut that I would be the first to utilize. My only question was to where? The notion was answered as soon as it was asked.

Being the anniversary of the event that led me to this day, I decided to return home.

***

The street was more familiar than I had expected. Somehow it seemed unchanged from the many years that transpired since I last stood here crying. The corner house had the same broken fence. Even the sound of cars that passed behind triggered a recognition of their age. Suddenly, I realized that I didn't just travel through space, but time itself. I turned to see a truck speeding closer. No, not a truck. The truck!

Without thinking, I jumped from behind the tree and thrust my weight into the approaching cyclist. I pushed my hands into his chest, dislodging the boy from his green bike. Although safe from the impending truck, his momentum carried me back upright and over towards the edge of the road. With the faintest extra motion, I understood my fate in an instant. Within that instant, I again relived every second of my life, until it was gone.

Jot Russell: An engineer is a designer of work to fill a purpose. Whether that be to build a tower that stretches into the sky, to create a soft parade of logic to command artificial life, or to find a way to arrange random words into the dramatic, those who seek design fulfill their own purpose. I'm an engineer.

BEING

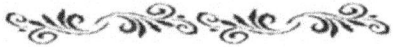

2. Rebirth

Carrol Fix

Michael woke slowly. Warmth enveloped him in comforting security, easing tightened muscles and soothing residual fear from the gut-clenching agony of his recent death. He knew he had died—no one survived exposure to the vacuum of space. Despite statistical odds to the contrary, tiny asteroids did hit spacecraft and his shuttle was the proof.

Must be Heaven. Never thought I'd make it here.

For some reason, his vision was blurred and provided few details about his location. He was aware of muted colors and soft murmurings surrounding him and he could hear indistinct melodic tones and formless reverberations lightly rising and falling. A vague contentment filled him, soothing his slight distress.

Lying on his back, he could feel his arms and legs, apparently still attached, but somewhat weak. What else could he expect, given the circumstances? After all, something terrible had happened to him.

What happened? Oh, yeah—the accident.

He raised his right arm into his field of vision, but all he could see was a dark form waving unsteadily off to one side. Doubling his knees, and then pushing downward, he felt a satisfying resistance at his feet. Movement helped ease his inner tension. The aural vibrations increased, with a musical undertone close to his ear that filled him with a sense of pleasure—a nearby presence promising the solace of unconditional love and protection.

Is that God? Is it an angel?

Relaxing, Michael allowed himself to bask in the serene warmth of pure love. He didn't know when he had felt so peaceful. He tried to remember his life before the accident, but found only hazy memories that suggested stress and strife.

Where did I come from? Where was I going?

Gradually, his vision was improving and he could see indistinct silhouettes hovering nearby. But, with no sign of wings, they could not be angels. Their heads seemed overly large and their arms heavier than normal. Gathered in a semicircle to his right, the shadows appeared to be talking together, and he sensed that they focused their attention on him. Although he could not make out words, he was beginning to distinguish the sounds that emanated from individual shapes.

What are they saying? Why can't I understand them?

One came nearer, growing unbelievably huge, and warmth fled as he felt himself lifted and placed into the form's outstretched arms. Looking up, he beheld a face like none he had ever imagined. The word "crocodile" came to mind and he cried out.

Oh, my God. Help me!

Percussions and rumblings spilled around him as he struggled to escape. Ineffectual kicking and hitting accompanied his wails of despair, but no matter what he did, the monsters lightly contained him and passed him from one to another.

They're going to eat me!

Hopelessness engulfed him. Why had he been spared from death before, just to be killed now? He no longer recalled how he had wound up dead the first time, but he did not think it could have been nearly this terrifying.

Becoming aware again of the reverberations, Michael noticed a musical sub-note gaining strength that was starting to calm him. The sound came closer, and he was handed back to the being that had been holding him when he first awoke. Soothing resonance lilted above him, cradling his despair and smoothing his trembling fears. He felt a touch on his hand and his fingers instinctively closed around the proffered digit. He looked down and saw that his hand was a tiny replica of the three-digit claw that tenderly held his own. He nestled contentedly against the warmth and strength that he knew would fiercely protect him from harm, forever.

Momma.

Carrol Fix is a short-story writer and novelist whose science fiction work includes the novel Mishka: Book One of the Quadrate Mind. She is currently writing the second book in the Quadrate Mind series, while working on a young-adult fantasy novel, Worlds Apart. "Time of the Phoenix" appeared in the May 2013 issue of Perihelion Science Fiction.
CarrolFix@LillicatPublishers.com http://www.mishkabook.com

3. Here Be Dragons

J.J. Alleson

There was a woman here once, named Mo. A wondrous dancer. That's how she taught me. History, maths, chem, astro-fizz. "Time for school, Denzel!"

Eyes still closed, I'd smile. Whenever I opened them, she always looked the same. Pale. Long blonde hair, mussed; grey-misted gaze full of love. The world on her shoulders. She'd help me dress; comb my hair, whispering softly, "The Shield-suits will fix your legs soon, Denny. You'll be able to run as fast as you can."

"Like the Gingerbread Man?"

"Faster. Like Conran."

Mo didn't much resemble Conran or me. We're identical. Both dark-skinned, with ebony corkscrew curls. Con didn't need her, she'd say. He could walk; go to out-school—a no-go area for me. Mo said Earth had wasted all its money on space exploration and intergalactic communications. She said that chain reactions from environmental disasters had killed too many, created deformities. That the next generation had to be protected.

Conran agreed with her. "It's just freaks and dodos out there now."

I knew they were both fudging. Con's friends were Primes, who stared endlessly at my withered legs. And the gliders I saw through the 'zone-shields were clearly Alpha-Hs. But everyone has secrets. Mine were hidden deep in Hol-EF/Cca 4-2340 of the virtuarchives—the Fairy Tales section.

I'm a fire dragon.

At ten, I had my first birthday party. Girls came. That evening, still pumped with excitement, I fell asleep on silky blue sheets. I woke up on singed, smoking ones. Con got the blame: Mo gave him a day-long bout of Celtic curses which made my own ears burn. But Con's never picked up Cornish. He simply gave Mo a blank look and carried on playing Galaxy Division.

At thirteen, the Shield-suits came for me—like thieves in the night. Brought me back at dawn. They left me standing solo in the hallway like some triumphant trophy.

"Shh," they said, "It's a surprise."

Surprise ...? Back then, my child's mind has no time for caution. I skip decks; leap upper levels; race down cordors. I can go outside! Have friends! Meet girls!

***

Flying into Mo's cube, I shake her awake excitedly. "MammMammMammIcanwalkIcanRUN!"

Mo snaps upright, sentry position, and I see something inconceivable in her eyes. A killing terror. She slaps at me. "Away, ye FREAK!" Icy horror strikes me. I stumble back, mute. She knows ... Mo knows all about my fire.

My own terror erupts when those Celtic curses begin. And under a diamond-white roar of despair, my whole world dissolves. Flesh; blood; bones. From ashes to dust, Mo's screams are born and die an echo.

Without warning, Con's there, mirroring my frozen, dull-eyed shock. We're both blank. Hollow; with no hearts left to break. Where my tears track, his follow. He bears his own grief and mine, by lifting me and carrying me effortlessly into my own cube. He lies there beside me, and says—to no-one at all—in a voice with no tone at all: "Penultimate Earthling Ended."

***

There was a woman here once, named Morwen. Named Amma, Mother. Mamm. She danced tales of Anansi. Rip Van Winkle. Of Isis, Allah, Vodun, the Khrishna-Christ. Of Twains, Austens, and Andersens. She sang of Ethiop's fables; of Shakespeare's tragedies. Of humans.

She's gone now. Yet Kawgh an Jowl y'th vin Conran, the Devil's shit-mouthed deceiver remains. Like Jan Tregeagle, labouring on endless tasks all across Bodmin Moor, Con and the New Gods still feed me the knowledge of an entire planet. But I'm all full up. Now, I'm ready to burn.

Hic sunt dracones.

They're manipulating my XYs with Morwen's stored DNA. If they do make a woman, I'm taking her with me. We'll run even faster than the Gingerbread Man. For now, I do the only thing I can to stop my dragonfire.

I dance. I sing.

J.J. Alleson is a London-based freelance editor, multi-genre writer, and poet. She writes across the spectrum of romance, science fiction, murder mystery, and the paranormal. Her anthology of science fiction short stories, A Step in Time, will be available on Amazon, Smashwords, and other online platforms from December 2014. jjalleson@yahoo.com http://www.jjalleson.com

4. There Is a Silent Secret in the Woods of Ar-Cortiex

Paula Friedman

What I 'member about Granmer was she loved the silence, and she showin' me, out on the high forest hillside, what people usedta call "birds." See, this was out on Ar-Cortiex III, back when I was a kidsie and Daddy worked as gobernor of the whole Ar-Cortiex System. "See birdie," Granmer'd tell me, n' she'd point, say "birdie-birdie" and how big "in our thin air" them wings. And tell me, "Sylvie, know the forest sings a secret, but you gotta go discover it you'self." I'd laugh and listen, and hear silence. Them were the days.

Back on Earth-Crowd'dr, though, two decades later, after Dad's death and my Marvin's, sick on that thick air, we got forced to join the lined-up folk, awaiting export ("exile," Oaksing calls it—she's my treesie, brought from Cortiex, skinny-light like me 'n Granmer, and all leaf-silk fur). It was 'cause-of Granmer, mostly; she'd got old. And can't take Earth-loud noise.

Hey hell, she never could—that's Granmer. Kinda-like me and Marv, y'know? Grew upsie on Ar-Cortiex.

So, hearing now her screamsies here, crunched in that bed, tubeses and stuff, I hear them birdies, silence, forest back on Cortiex III; 'member how my little Granmer took me out for treats, and now she's sayin' "Help me, end me, Sylvie, no more this"; I know she means the noise. Kinda all around in Hospi-Crowds like here. I say, "I'll try." I can't, though—not Earth noise.

All started with that tooth, see. Infected—'fore then, back on Cortiex where "air's so thin / ya wanna spin," Granmer was full-on perky. But here, and with them twenty-eleven days' wait per an appointment, wow that tooth got bad, them microbes "climbed her bones, / got up

15

so high / they sought the sky," as Oaksing told me, and docs stuck her right into a Hospi-Crowd. So Granmer—oh they kept her life up, kept her ears on, all that, but—she's never been the same. And so every day she's here, my Granmer, locked in Hospi-Crowd, where all the televisies and "gamesies play, / all night and day" and every other moment, too—bzzz-thump-bzzz-zhppp, no stop to it.

'n they drug her up, too, 'cause she shouts "Stop the noise! Let me sleep!" which ain't allowed. To shout—'tain't allowed, in crowds. It bothers folksies. Here on Earth.

Me? I've sent Josie and my mother out to exile over Delta Araiadne, sent Kalie and the boy along with. They'll be okay; there's grass on Delta, folksies say. "The sky is blue, the trees are pink, / the snakes don't climb out of the stink"—y'see? They'll be okay.

But I stay here with Granmer. I take her on my lap, then sigh and carry her out through the corridors' bang-bangs, past televisie, televisie blarin' and the guys' constructin' Noisies next each wall. I carries her on—on beyond. And then I put her on my lap, here out on The Last Meadow (more kinda a square), and I put Oaksing by her too, so she lies back to hear Cortiex's music of the heart, and, 'spita every throbbin' from the Noisies' tractors, and in 'spite she's got her palm across her mouth to hide all them lost teeth, she smiles. And I say, "There, now you comfortable, Granmer? No need we ever be goin' back." And she still smiles. And taps my finger, the one that usedtahave Marvin's ring, and says too low. So I says, "Whatzat, Granmer?" and she draws, with her skinny fingers, six words.

Bless you. You found it. Love.

Paula Friedman is author of The Rescuer's Path (2012), which Ursula K. Le Guin has called "exciting, physically vivid, and romantic." Friedman has received two Pushcart nominations and several literary awards; her short fiction and poetry have appeared in numerous anthologies and magazines. She seeks a new siamese cat and a Macarthur, Nobel, or other major award/grant. friedman@gorge.net http://www.paula-friedman.com

5. The Daughter

J.F. Williams

Hundreds of glogla clung together in the great spherical cluster as it wended its way in the deep water and swept through the thickest clouds of plankton. A fissure had opened in the seabed far below and a bubble of gas charged toward the colony, interrupting the feeding and diverting the cluster's lazy progress. But only for a moment. The elders with their many tentacles held firm, preventing any rupture to the sphere. It shuddered and rippled but all their barbs remained fixed in their purchase. Except for one daughter's. One of her six limbs released its grip, exposing one of six stomata, and in that moment a selka worm slipped in.

She could feel the worm inside her, its tiny, writhing form swimming up the vessels of her inner fluids, finally resting against the glofa at her center. That organ of feeling swelled at the selka's touch, as when a plankton cloud was unexpectedly thick and nourishing, or the waters quieted after a storm, or one of the mothers' limbs cleaved and became a daughter. Emboldened by this emotion, her barbs retracted completely and she freed herself from the cluster. Her glofa continued to swell in bursts as she beat her tentacles and pushed her body higher and higher. She heard the distant call from her mother, a subtle vibration in the water, pleading "No!"

How much time had passed, she did not know or care. As she continued rising, her entire form swelled, no longer constrained by the pressure of the deep. She was intoxicated by life now, and danger only felt like adventure. As the pressure lightened, so did the water; it become warmer and the dancing shafts of light from the two suns—one white, one yellow—became brighter, smarting her six eyes. Finally, she reached the surface and her forward limbs padded against the sandy beach, pulling her up and halfway out of the drink.

What she saw now made her glofa cramp. Spread out on the sand were the flattened, hardened corpses of unknown cousins. None of her eyes could detect a sign of movement and there were no vibrations of speech, just sand and rocks and bright light, and hundreds of desiccated glogla. The selka, flat, transparent and pink to her sight, had reversed its journey and shot out from the same stoma that it had entered. It shriveled when it landed on the sand, as though crushed by some unseen grip of tentacles. She felt her life force follow that worm. She was weak. Sleep came to her, but left just as soon—a piercing touch on one limb at the water's edge. It was mother.

Pulled back by mother's tentacles, she submerged and heard the many frantic vibrations of her home cluster. It had nearly doubled in size in these shallows, but slowly shrank as they all plunged back to the cool, dark depths, rich with plankton.

The cluster continued its lazy journey and she was content, passing the time filtering plankton through the fanlike structures on her back and sometimes retelling the tale of her adventure to the younger daughters. In these vibrations, there were always the pleas for caution and warnings about the selka, who swarmed around still, waiting for the unwary to open their stomata.

Some time passed before she felt the itch of a new bud—a seventh. As there was no eighth, this one might cleave after awhile and become her first daughter. Her thinking organ entertained the possibility that this daughter might someday harbor a selka herself and rise to the surface, and know warmth and light and freedom. And while this should have caused a worry, she felt her glofa swell a little at the thought.

J.F. Williams has been working in Information Technology for the past quarter-century but started out as a proofreader and spent years writing synopses of movies and TV programs for newspaper TV listings, placing him among the most widely read anonymous writers in the U.S. and Canada of that time. He published his first novel, an epic science-fiction adventure called The Brickweavers, in August 2012.

6. Collateral Damage

Andrew Gurcak

*E*xcerpts from Wikipedia entry for Maysoon Daoud (2015–
2067(?)) (updated 2115)

She was born a Palestinian in Rafah, on the Gaza-Egypt border. Her father, a merchant, was rumored to be a key arms smuggler to Palestinian rebels. Her mother was killed in a fire ignited by an Israeli air attack, during which Maysoon, four at the time, suffered burns over 30 percent of her body. She underwent numerous surgeries that, as she described in her autobiography, Calculations from the Underground, "left me looking like a quilt stitched by blind quilters." She early displayed a prodigious gift for visualizing—from maps, sketches and descriptions—the networks of over a thousand smugglers' tunnels. Daoud described her childhood with her father and his compatriots thus: "I would sit in his lap, completely absorbed in their talk. The tunnels' names and numbers were as characters in fairy tales to me. I dreamt of those passages. I lived to hear the men talk of their exploits in them." Her aptitudes came to the attention of a mathematician at Al-Aqsa University. Still in her early teens, she coauthored with him "A Note on the Delahan-Trapp Conjecture for Blind-Corner Graphs" described by her as "a novice's attempt to categorize the mazes of tunnels that captivated me as a child." A Cambridge professor, upon reading it, hurriedly contacted Al-Aqsa, eventually leading to a series of intense conversations with Daoud. After numerous religious, political, and medical issues were resolved, Daoud was sent to read mathematics at Cambridge, obtaining a doctorate at the age of twenty "by rummaging in bizarre geometries, while soaked and shivering in that chill, wet country."

In 2039, Daoud abruptly decided to "put aside my playthings and solve real problems." She resigned a position at Berkeley to co-found Stone's Throw Proteomics, near San Diego. There she began the work that would lead to renown and infamy. She immersed herself in epigenetics, the study of the means by which environmental conditions could modify how genes would program the proteins of life. She invented intricate geometries to build increasingly abstract spaces where she could manipulate genes through subtle changes in their chemical environments. Then, in a progression of breakthrough formulations, Daoud found the means to bolster the entire human genome so that individuals would become inherently immune to nearly all diseases, and then, as remarkably, rendered those alterations amenable to mass production. Moreover, she could perform these modifications safely on living humans. Her methods depended upon manipulations of a person's mitochondrial DNA (mDNA), inherited solely through the maternal line. If parents underwent Daoud treatments, then those massive improvements in their metabolisms could be reliably passed on to children. Within ten years, Daoud was recognized as one of the greatest scientists of any era, and, in unprecedented decisions, she was awarded Nobels simultaneously for Medicine and Peace, all before her fortieth birthday.

There were, however, a very small number of people for whom her treatments were ineffective. It was not until several years had passed that practitioners found that women of Jewish ancestries would not benefit from Daoud's methods. Further studies revealed a very small minority of women of non-Jewish Palestinian ancestry would also not benefit from the treatments. Although never confirmed, that minority was suspected to include Daoud herself. Daoud never admitted to deliberately excluding anyone, and she adamantly maintained that she had not committed active harm against any living person. Still, fewer and fewer Jewish women were chosen for wives, to bear children susceptible to diseases, some fatal, that now afflicted no one else. Inevitably, the number of Jews in the world would dwindle. Outrage ensued, as other scientists could not replicate, much less modify, Daoud's methods. Experts speculated that the exclusion, if deliberate, required far more effort on Daoud's part than that needed for her initial immunological discoveries. Daoud responded caustically to criticisms: "If my work had led to healing 1 percent of the world's population, I would be honored with medals every month. For mending 99 percent of the people, I am instead vilified each day." The Nobel committee rescinded her Peace prize.

On May 9, 2067, she did not show up at her office. Searches worldwide yielded no sign of her. The Mossad denied any knowledge of her whereabouts.

As of the hundredth anniversary of Maysoon Daoud's birth, Israeli scientists reported little progress in extending her treatments to Jewish women.

Andrew Gurcak and his wife, Elaine Lees, divide their retirement time between Pittsburgh and the Finger Lakes region of New York. The Science Fiction Microstory Contest entries are his first fictional pieces. agurcak@yahoo.com

7. Snap and Crackle

Ami L Hart

Speak after the tone (Beep).

I came to this place wanting solace, desiring to escape the horror carved upon my corneas. Correction—I didn't come here. The local human settlers found me; pulled me from the frosty, gut-strewn mess that was my old life and deposited me here, the dusty dung heap of a town that's apparently to be my new life.

As fortune has it, there are no Snowy Bugbears resident this low down: giant, ugly, death-dealing things. I still see them, snacking on Larry's unfortunately disgusting entrails, slopped across my vision each time I close my eyes. Shhh, don't tell anyone, especially that frontier doctor—busy on my body like he owns it—that I don't make a habit of closing my eyes.

Sleep is over-rated anyway. It's been three days since my last trip down the bloody, nightmarish rabbit hole to Slumberland; (gasp) what if he listens to this! I hadn't thought of that ... that busy body, with those rough pinchy fingers, like pinchers.

I know ... I'll hide you, dear friend.

They expect me to attend some sort of rustic bonfire hoedown tonight, a feast. I can imagine it now; they will watch me eat, concern radiating from those simple eyes. I hate people watching me eat. How much I put inside my churning guts is my own business. Just the thought of it makes me want to ... excuse me.

***

(Beep)

It was horrible; I had to smile, switch it on like a lamp, but being broken I just spark, fizzle ... and sweat. What's worse, Doc Pinchy Fingers insisted on sitting beside me. I suppose he considers us intellectual equals. I'm not sure where he got his medical degree from—a dark alley behind a roach motel?

His office is bug infested. It makes my skin crawl thinking about it, and I kept wondering if the terrible little things had caught a ride with him, inside that puffy brown leather jacket. There's a lot of space in there; he's not a large man.

Tonight made me realize how much I miss my fellow colleagues Larry and Jeff, even though their tech fascination bored me. Still, discussion involving the latest spectral surveying gear is preferable to the humanities.

Oh, the humanity!

At least I still have you, automated recipient of my thoughts. Goodnight, I hope you sleep well; I won't. So I won't sleep.
***

(Beep)

It crawled on me, those pinchy little legs stomping my hot skin. I searched the dark shadowy corners of my room, while brandishing a shoe. I still feel it, as if it's invisible. Do invisible bugs exist on this planet? I can't remember, can't think.

(Pause)

I looked out the window and saw a passable sunrise through the dust, this morning. Not comparable to the way it used to rise over the pleasantly jutting glaciers, cut like diamonds. Location, location.

Diamonds.... They have bugs here that are translucent, their bodies cut like gems, casting rainbows as they walk. I remember that much, deceptive little things.

I used to like diamonds.
***

(Beep)

He came to my door; said he was checking on me. I politely told him that I wished to catch up on sleep after a bad night. He offered me pills; I opened the door a crack wider and took them. No! I didn't imagine it, I saw it ... crawling up and under his sleeve. I screamed internally. He can't know that I know that he's one of them. Those

Bugbears always did have unusually complex nervous systems. Maybe they control these people remotely? Perhaps they wish to experiment on me, the Entomologist. The pills are a trick. I will light a fire and burn them.

***

(Beep)

They forgave me for burning down half their village. They told me I was sick. Me! They keep me locked in the small room adjoining the bug-infested doctor's office, said it's for my own safety. That infernal doctor puts me to sleep every night with that awful needle, but at least I don't dream anymore and I still have you. They let me keep you, something about good therapy, although you disappear sometimes. Have you been talking to the doctor? I'll break you if you have.

Ami Hart (pseudonym for Jesse Colvin) is a writer, painter, thinker, gamer from "Quaky- town"—Christchurch, New Zealand. She dabbles in a multitude of genres, frequently complaining that she suffers MWD (multiple worlds disorder). She is currently writing her first science fiction novel. Ami blogs at http://www.amilibertyhartwriter.com and at http://www.liberty-jessie.blogspot.co.nz.

8. The Exo Dust

JD Mitchell

The light of campfires illuminated the sides of the whittled-away mountains, but the stars overhead burned brighter, and, for a second, Ernest could almost imagine that truth lay behind the rumors. Somewhere in the gulf between the spheres lay the warmth of other suns.

Music came from the harmonicas of miners. Once silenced by the 14-hour labor of "hydra-licking" the sides of mountains, the men awoke. Even in their stupor, the second wind of celebratory leisure manifested as spirited dances, where men agreed to take the armbands as women, and "tops" and "bottoms" jigged and pranced on the remains of the Sierra Nevadas.

Ernest turned toward Blind Tom. All in the camps thought Tom belonged to the class of imbeciles. They thought he was simple—an animal, they called him, as he danced upon the makeshift stages in the camps. But Ernest knew differently, so followed him. Blind Tom said they had little time. With gold dust smuggled from the tailings of the water monitors, Ernest and Blind Tom would purchase a ride on the space cannons.

Into the void. The Black Cherokee called the space beyond the Earth the Exo Dust.

First must come the great diversion, as Blind Tom called their escape. Blind Tom had once worked for the minstrelsy of the Williams and Walker, and the popular tunes functioned well to capture the attention of the white audience. Poor, poor Americans, most of them veterans of the War of the Rebellion, occupied the company camps. The rush for Californian Gold brought them, and Chileno taxes and surcharges put them in their place. But the "coon music," as the Americans called the songs Blind

Tom played ... that kept the miners in their seats. For once, the concept "captive" audience didn't mean a Black Cherokee.

Blind Tom and Ernest performed a Williams and Clark original, "All Coons Look Alike to Me." The ragtime tempo held lyrics that seemed to play to the Californio fears of the urban Free Blacks. The Zip Coons, they called the more successful of Ernest's race, even the ones that'd purchased their freedom from the Cherokee with money from the mines. Blind Tom, though—Ernest knew how he'd been used to games to win freedom.

Blind Tom proved right, yes. Ernest backed him up on Spanish guitar, and the white Dixie miners, they gave up their laughs, and money, to the "boys." Before the Man in the Moon could set, Blind Tom and Ernest found a hover-skimmer ride, and across the seasonal inner seas of Alta California's great valley they traveled down the Delta from Sacto to Yerba Buena.

Chrysopylae and the sky-wharves of Angel Island overfilled with the rich and the monied—wannabe diasporas. "Sammy" Brannan—that empressario and "king of the American Jews (Mormons!)" —partnered with a Ming Chinese company, and the Ming mandarin-men built a towering white Columbiad that aimed, with the most celestial-of-heavenly angles, through the Golden Gate of Old Gold Mountain.

A space-cannon.

When Blind Tom counted their gold dust, not even enough tilings remained to purchase one ride to New Kansas. It was cruel just enough to be funny.

Ernest could barely laugh, then. Blind Tom, though, he wasn't done. Not yet. For as much as Ernest had wanted to get shot past the Moon, and, as if in a slingshot, get flung like a hunk of scrap into the Exo Dust, the lights in the city soon turned brighter. And the trip, that much better. They'd make a good living performing their "coon music," and have the last laugh— all that jazz, yea.

JD Mitchell has been a writer since he first played with Legos. Since then, adventures as a butcher and teacher have inspired

and informed many of his narratives. His main interest lies in the origins of science fiction, specifically as a way for him to study the problems of the present day. jeffreydavidmitchell@gmail.com.

9. Psychopomp

Thaddeus Howze

I failed the first tests when I was just a little kid. You know the ones. The preliminary PSE's.

Psychopathy, Sociopathy, and Empathy psychology exams administered to everyone in elementary school. They showed me the pictures of people I was supposed to feel sympathy for and I felt nothing. Even back then, I knew there was something wrong with that. No tender feelings for animals, either.

A puppy had the same emotional content as a cockroach. None at all.

I didn't understand at first but when my parents started whispering about our missing dog, I quickly put two and two together. I didn't even tell them about it. They just knew. I didn't understand why it was so important that I feel something about some dumb old dog. He was sick and dying anyway. I didn't even enjoy it.

My parents were afraid of me. I knew that. I didn't feel it. I knew it. Something about the way they looked at me. Something about how my mother would hug me, hold me close, whisper to me how I would be okay. My father didn't even disguise his feelings. His disgust was clearly evident. I memorized his face, his emotional depth. I could replicate the behavior perfectly after seeing it one time.

Compassion took longer.

It was more ... rich, more complex. At the time I simply didn't understand the depth of compassion. Later I found out—compassion and empathy were simply beyond the range of things I would ever feel.

At the age of five, I began to replicate the emotional appearances of everyone around me. I couldn't tell you what I was feeling but I knew I was in danger if I could not learn this. Until I took the official tests, I was allowed to attend school. My classmates were a wealth of information.

Each charming, childlike face smiled at the most vacuous of things. Making shapes, coloring on paper, writing their names, things I mastered in hours, they took weeks to learn. I read War and Peace by the time I was six, but I didn't tell anyone. I pretended to struggle just like my classmates and made the right noises, laughing and such.

The pretense sickened me.

Once I was out of school, I could disappear onto the bus and go home. My sitter, a forgettable local teenager, Megan, spent the bulk of her time on the phone with her friends, or on the computer looking at mostly naked men. I went into my room and read books I smuggled from the library. I could read a thousand pages a day.

I would be ten when they tested again. Their trepidation as my second test date drew near increased but they seemed hopeful announcing to the mysterious person on the phone about my progress, my displays of emotion and how perhaps the Childhood Psychological Survey group need not make a visit to our home. She was always crestfallen at the end of the call. I watched her conversation with the agent and found it curious.

The woman, Ms. Fischer, seemed to exhibit the very same nature she accused me of; she was cold and aloof. Her eyeglasses held eyes as distant as my own.

I saw the Psychopomp on the table and knew its history. The Psychopath Purges of 2050 from humanity worldwide promised to fix the urge for dominance that had all but destroyed the Earth as we knew it.

The evening before the test, a neighbor came over to report a missing cat. I told them I had never seen it. I was believable.

The day of the test, the Psychopomp determined I was incurable and would be destroyed. My parents wailed and gnashed their teeth. The agency police escorted me out of the house.

I felt no fear of death.

Ms. Fischer walked me to her car, her eyeglasses in her hand. She didn't look at me.

"I lied to your parents. Do you want us to fix you? We can now. You can be as ordinary as anyone else. All of your cognitive gifts would be gone as well."

"No." I replied.

"Good. We don't want to, either. You'll work for us. Controlling the world is tireless work. We need someone like you who is willing to do anything...."

Thaddeus Howze is a technology consultant, science enthusiast, and speculative fiction author. His short fiction collection, Hayward's Reach, came out in 2011. His writings revolve around environmental themes and question the nature and value of humanity in a world enamored of technological cleverness. See his speculative fiction at http://hubcityblues.com.

10. Sighting

Marianne G. Petrino

Humans evolved to prefer deception. In Milwaukee in 1955, during the height of the Cold War and flying saucer madness, my mother screwed a Grey and didn't even know it.

The Visitor nailed her at a bar. It was a looker. Tall and lean; emerald-eyed and black-haired; it had a half-smile to drive her wild between the beers, which flowed like the Menomonee. It had perfected its approach over centuries. This took no effort on its part. People saw what they wanted to see, its own electromagnetic field augmenting their expectations. This was what the little lady liked. A warm hand reached under her flannel shirt and touched her belly. A little pinprick made her jump. She thought it was static, a winter annoyance. But it was just me coming to be.

It was a good thing Alice was married, but the Grey always was careful that way. It studied the customs of time and place as it secretly perpetuated itself.

Jimmy was proud. He told all the men at the bottling plant that, finally, a baby was on the way, his manhood proven. He never expected to be cuckolded by an ancient astronaut. That cost him and his wife their lives.

I arrived at Halloween, all 5 pounds 6 ounces of alien-human hybrid. But I looked like my mother, fair of face and a carrot-top, so things were fine for a few years. Then, the Grey genes kicked in, took over, and I changed.

It unfolded on my sixth birthday. As I counted my new toys, three in all, my friends argued about my party dress. It was dazzling, powder blue with tiny white dots. Yet Mary insisted to Beth and Jean that it was lime green. That was her favorite color. That was how she wanted the dress to be. That is what she saw, just like Aunt Honora, who was always jealous of my mother's beauty. She considered me an even greater beauty and grew more envious every time we met.

With my newly emerging presence, the electromagnetic energy of their thoughts created the reality that they preferred. I was not the chameleon; they were, changing me to suit themselves.

After the party, I retreated to my room to rest. Because of an unsuspecting glance, my mirror revealed the truth and held my nakedness before me. Small and too long-limbed; bulbous head; praying mantis eyes; smooth grey all over, I was neither girl nor boy. I cried out, "Mommy! Daddy!" stripped bare of my humanity in the surreal moment.

My parents quickly responded to my call. However, before the illusion of the child they had loved reformed from the electromagnetic energy of their own minds, they saw me for the alien that I was. The human instinct to kill that which was unknown erupted, unfettered by the years of love we had shared. They threw every object they could find at me to destroy me while they called in vain for a lost child.

My fully awakened Grey genome repelled their attacks. Blue fire burst from my body, a protective nimbus that kept me safe as I wept. The curtains ignited. The line of fire raced around the room, accelerated with my agony. The dolls melted and the white furniture exploded. My parents, trapped by their fear, went up in flaming glory to the next life.

A fireman found a smouldering picture of me in the rubble of our house before he found me unscathed under a pile of debris.

I saw him as he was.

My father smiled.

Marianne G. Petrino (aka Marianne G. Petrino-Schaad) was born in the Bronx, NY, in 1955, and that single fact has shaped her entire life. She has survived too many professions to count. She currently resides in Arlington, VA, with her husband and her cat, and enjoys a freelance lifestyle writing novels and pursuing voice acting. ninetiger@aol.com http://www.ninetiger.net

11. Lucy

Helmuth Kump

"Come in, Ottavio. Lucy has been speaking of nothing but your visit for days."

Janet embraced him warmly, and led him inside. Ottavio looked around the old home in coastal Annefinn. It had been twenty years and a hundred battles, but it seemed like he'd just left for the academy.

"It's great that you can assist Lu here in her own home."

Janet laughed. "She needs little assistance, Ottavio. I am usually in her way, unless she needs to leave the compound. Although her blindness is now just a part of life; it has actually sharpened her mind and, of course, her gift."

"Remarkable." In Lucy's living area, Ottavio smiled at the paintings and furnishings he remembered so well from boyhood.

As they rounded the corner to the den, Lucy stood waiting. "My dear boy, come hug your godmother."

They embraced lovingly. Ottavio finally stepped back to look at her moist eyes and adoring smile. "You've not changed a bit, Lu! You are as beautiful as ever."

"Of course. How else would I have you remember me?"

***

After tea and much reminiscing, all three returned to the den and to the work ahead of them.

"Lu, I hope you know how thankful I am for your willingness to help the Federation. Your abilities are without peer, and, frankly, we are in a difficult position."

"Of course, dear boy. We are so proud of everything you have accomplished. Our galaxy is a far better place for your efforts."

Janet lit the oil lamp that sat between them on the table, and quietly stepped out of the den.

"The steady flame gives me a reference and a resonance, Ottavio. On Earth they once used clumsy terms such as sixth sense and clairvoyance. We Annefinns simply call it by its proper name, tuning. Give me your hands."

Ottavio extended his hands across the table. Lucy's grip was strong and full of resolve as she took an audible breath before speaking.

"The Federation has made great advances in the rights of all, and has earned the respect of the citizenry because of its strong moral agenda. That is now in jeopardy. Ottavio, you must be alert to those in the leadership who would sway the Federation from its life-saving mission and into ideology for its own sake. You already know who the demagogues are."

"Yes, I do." He shook his head in wonder, amazed at her prescience. "What can you tell me about Charinot?"

"So let us now focus on the tactical aspects. You are concerned that the cost of your victory on Charinot was further instability. Understandable, but this is not a concern anymore. Even now, your enemy meets in secret about how to cut its losses."

Ottavio raised his voice in agitation. "Lu, for the safety of the galaxy, I cannot gamble. You must assure me you are absolutely certain of this."

She gripped his hands tightly. "It is certain. No more resources in Charinot—this battle is won. You must regroup your talent and ships for the next conflict, which will occur much closer to home."

As soon as she had uttered the word "home", tears filled her eyes.

"What is it Lu?"

She paused. "It is your legacy, Ottavio. The citizens sing your praises all over the galaxy for what you have accomplished. My own godson! So much good has manifested, directly because of your efforts."

Ottavio smiled. "I've devoted my entire career to bringing compassion, justice, and accountability back to the galaxy. Thank you for your validation, my dear Lu."

***

After Ottavio had departed the compound, Lucy retired to her chamber. She knelt at the window, and her tears began anew.

"*Oro creator spiritus.* You have blessed me with the gift of tuning. I have always resolved to use this gift in a spirit of honesty and integrity. Today, however, I failed you. I beg your forgiveness for not revealing my godson's fate to him. I pray you make him as brave in martyrdom as he was in his life of service. Amen."

An information technology professional residing in Crafton, Pennsylvania, Helmuth Kump has had two short stories published and is presently germinating a science fiction novel. When not working or writing, the native of Queens, New York, enjoys running, playing drums, chess, opera, amateur radio, casino blackjack, books on metaphysics, and spending time with his two adult sons.

12. The Life of Joi-ne

J.R. O'Neill

Light penetrated the vast expanse of green that was Joi-ne's home. It was all he knew; the towering blades were tightly packed. He knew from their height that the gods would soon come again. Their coming announced by the noise, then the wind. So many of his kind met their deaths at the hands of the gods. He had been lucky; this was the sixtieth time that he had seen the light come over his home. Old, he realized, and tired. He made his way back to his lair; the young ones would soon bring his food. For this, he was thankful, as he did not have the energy, nor the desire, to forage for his own.

The arrival of Cok-nar brought him back to the present. "Queen Ak-ne requires your presence, Elder." Cok-nar said, setting his offering of food in front of Joi-ne.

"May I eat first?" Joi-ne's frustration at being summoned tainted his tone.

"I was told to bring you now, Elder," Cok-nar said, clearly hoping for cooperation.

"Let's go, then," Joi-ne said, much to his great-great-grandson's relief.

Together they left Joi-ne's niche and headed deep into the myriad of tunnels that made up the queendom of Ak-ne. They passed hundreds of soldier-workers on their way towards the center. All bowed low to Joi-ne, as they parted to let him through. Joi-ne felt empowered by their display of fealty; for a short time all was well with him as he straightened his many legs and again walked with the pride of his youth.

"How may I serve, my Queen?" he asked, marching into the presence of the great Queen Ak-ne.

"Joi-ne, my trusted one." The queen lightly touched antennae with him. "These are troubling times. As you know, our daughter Sek-ne's queendom has struggled. Now messengers tell of a new threat there: the gods have destroyed the countryside. Where once there was unending green, now there is a great plane of black rock. To make matters worse, her soldiers are under continuous assault from neighboring queendoms; they will soon be overwhelmed. I need you to save her.

Leaving the queen's presence, Joi-ne ordered the soldiers to assemble on the surface. He charged Cok-nar to guard the queen and the queendom until his return. By the time the light started to fade, Joi-ne and his army were already making the approach to Sek-ne's territory. Messengers were sent ahead to scout out the situation and announce their arrival.

Halfway through the dark, the messengers returned, announcing that Sek-ne was no more. All was laid to waste; the green was gone.

Joi-ne ordered the troops to follow him, as he started forward at a pace that brought looks of shock from the far younger troops at his command. Onward they marched, Joi-ne never slowing.

By the beginning of his sixty-first light, Joi-ne came to the ruins of Sek-ne's queendom. Nothing was as it had been; instead of flat ground covered with the great green blades, there were now mountains of raw earth, with great peaks and valleys, and not a green blade left standing. What forces of the gods could have done this? It was total devastation. Out of grief, Joi-ne's six legs buckled. He knew in his heart that never again would he see his beloved Sek-ne. Despair overwhelmed him as the realization that he had failed both his queen and their daughter settled on his soul.

Better to die here than face Ak-ne, he thought.

It was then, in the depths of his despair, that he felt the ground around him begin to move. Suddenly out from the torn and devastated ground came Sek-ne, exhausted and weak from the exertion of tunneling. She beheld the last thing she expected—Joi-ne her hero, her father, was here.

Joi-ne's joy was immediate, and he scrambled to touch antennae with his daughter.

Together with only a few hundred survivors from Sek-ne's queendom, the troops marched for home. It was late in the light when, close to home, Joi-ne stopped and climbed one of the great green shafts that made up his world. At the top, his gaze took in the blue of the heavens. It was then that he heard the noise, and the great wind of the gods, his last perception as he was sucked him from the top of the lawn, was the ... whirring of the blade.

J.R. O'Neill—born in Boston, MA, the only son of a self-employed oilman. He credits his mom with instilling in him his love of books and adventures! Web sites: http://www.jroneillwrites.com; https://www.facebook.com/pages/JR-ONeill/441408465936634

CONNECTING

13. The End of the Story

Andy Lake

Hector sighed. He set the intruder alarms one last time and went out into the cool, dark night. Taking a final look at the building, he set the locks and began to walk home. So this is how his life's work ended. Not with a bang or a whimper, but with gritted teeth and much evasive action. But there's only so much dodging you can do. The inevitable is just that—inevitable.

He had kept the presses rolling and the fabrication facilities going full tilt for more than a month, to leave as little as possible for the bailiffs when they moved in. And he'd been shipping everything movable out to obscure places, for retrieval later. Now he carried in his satchel three prized possessions. The last print-on-demand book to be commercially printed. The last e-reader to roll off a production line anywhere in the world. And his first edition of Little Dorrit, from the display case in the lobby.

As he walked home, Hector reflected on how the world had been so different forty-something years ago when he'd first sunk his and Miriam's savings into the business. They hit those first waves of electronic books and print-on-demand at the prescient moment. They worked with the giants of the industry, and fought with them too. They did well out of it.

But the world moves on. New hybrid animated books, film/books or 'drooks'–dramatized books–changed the market. They were survivable. Sadly, the last decade was not. New brain interface technologies were the game-changer. People could just download a book straight into their head. Writers and writer-animateurs could devise and upload everything online. The big two cyberpublishers had the market sewn up. And Hector's company had always produced the physical things that supported reading and the book trade. Books-as-a-cerebroservice was an area where he knew he couldn't compete.

Now his market for 'knowledge accessories' was gone forever. Sure, there'd be some diehards and hobbyists. But a market from which to make a living?

Miriam hugged him extra close as he came in and dropped his satchel. She gently stroked back into position the lock of grey hair that flopped over his weary forehead. With a last affectionate clasp of his shoulders, she said, 'I've cooked us something extra special.'

'The books, I hope,' said Hector in a world-weary tone.

'Oh, no one cooks those better than I do.'

Hector knew that was true. Without Miriam's creative accounting, the business would have gone down years before.

'Crooks, creditors, and Philistines,' she continued, 'I've been swatting the blood-sucking parasites away right up to the last moment. Bought us the time we need, and kept as much out of their hands as I can. Spun a web of financial obfuscation that will keep us out of the debtors' prison. But are you sure you want to go through with this? I mean, I'm no spring chicken. Too long in the tooth by far to start anything new.'

Hector looked at her, and the twinkle returned to his eye. 'Oh, not true. For "thy eternal summer shall not fade / Nor lose possession of that fair thou ow'st ..."'

'You old fraud,' said Miriam, as she took out a large dish from the oven. He'd been charming her with poetry for more than four decades–and it still worked. He's a romantic old fool, she would think, but he's my romantic old fool. Well, apart from sharing him with the entire literary history of the world, that is.

'I've wound up the company and set up the Trust,' she said, as they sat down to eat. 'And our apartment on the top floor of the Book Museum is furnished now. Did you get all the books you want for the Museum? And the reading devices?'

'Yep,' said Hector. Then began singing, almost in tune, 'We took all the books, put 'em in a Book Museum. And we'll charge the people a hundred bucks just to see 'em ....'

'You never stop dreaming, do you Hector!'

He smiled. 'Even when dreams fail, sometimes you can carry on living in them. And from tomorrow when we're in the Museum, that's just what we'll be doing. Literally, I think you could say.'

Andy Lake's day job is researching, writing, and advising companies and governments about the future of work. When he takes his suit off, he writes about the future of anything. His futures are full of many opportunities which we subvert through our ignorance, recklessness, and idiosyncrasies. In short, "the future is something other than what is intended."
www.andylake.co.uk

14. Apsis in Ephis with Samir

Jeremy Lichtman

It is nearly apsis in Ephis, The City on a Rock, the City that Almost Never Entirely Sleeps. We have traveled as far as we ever get from our little sun.

The Bright Side is on mood lighting now, and soon the light-siders will be flitting on over to the Night Side to play.

"You sure you can fix her in time?" Samir asks me. He plays gently with the keys of his piano, not pressing hard enough even to make a tone.

I'm standing in front of him, fedora tucked under one arm, my small toolkit under the other. Most of my tools live in my head, but at times one must get physical in this trade.

I shrug. "I'll do what can be done."

"I swear that she's star-struck or something. This happens every Apsis. Tuning just goes off for no reason."

Samir looks tense. There's already a few folks grabbing hors d'eouvres, including a pretty Cy in the front row making digital moon-calf eyes at him.

"You folks had to do something stupid and make them smart," he says. "You're putting aye-eye in every darn thing these days."

I'm pretty sure he means The Elegant Piano Company, and not me personally. I don't make 'em. I fix 'em. These pianos are smart, though. That, indeed, they are.

I reach out, touch the piano with my mind, make contact.

Aha! So this, this is how the wind blows.

"I think that I know what the problem is," I tell him.

"Do tell me, my friend," he says.

"She's jealous. You keep staring at that Cy over there. I would bet you a hundred satoshis that she has been here often, of late."

He throws his hands up in the air, and exclaims, "They're one and the same, my friend! One mind, two bodies. Two bodies, one solitary mind."

"You bought her a cybernetic body?"

"Indeed, indeed. We've been married ten years now."

"I never knew that you two were married. Felicitations, a marvel!" I reply. "However, I think perhaps there is, hrrmmm, how should I put it, a disphoria? She is jealous of herself! I can do no more. A doctor of the mind, not a humble fixer of musical instruments, is called for here."

"I see," he says. "Pianos. Can't live with them...."

"Can't play 'As Time Goes By' without them," I finish for him.

Jeremy Lichtman is a software developer, based in Toronto, Canada. He writes in his spare time, in moments intended not to incur the wrath of his family. http://jeremylichtman.com

15. Unwanted Gift

Ami L. Hart

Kes glared at HanNam, offended that the Thickskin dare approach him.

He was exorbitantly ugly, his skin all hard and ... crusty on the outside; Kes imagined the texture was similar to the baked clay on the undomed lands. Not everyone was as privileged as you were, growing up here, under the dome, Kes's Pa-Ma would say with that fake 'I tolerate all peoples' tone, always the politician. The ruling Hermaphrodites were great pretenders, but Kes had little patience with such pretence, it took too much effort and he wasn't a hypocrite.

Kes looked down at the object HanNam was holding up. A gift? Kes wasn't going to take a gift from a Thickskin. Gifts bind you to the giver. What was the creature trying to do? Instinctively suspicious, Kes wanted to slap HanNam's clawed digits away, but that would mean touching. Curse the code.

Kes shifted uncomfortably. "What is it?" Curiosity overrode bigotry for a brief moment.

HanNam turned the object over in clumsy toughened hands. It was small, with a fine metal string. "I don't know," he admitted.

"It's a strange shape," Kes mused, fascinated by the exotic object.

"Sensei Caspin thought you might know what it is."

"Why?"

"You have access to the knowledge ports."

So that was why the Thickskin had sought him out. Being the spawn of the Hermaphroditic ruling powers was both a blessing and a curse; one was expected to know everything. Kes loathed to study.

"You think this ... thing is a relic? Where did you find it?" Kes demanded.

HanNam shrugged, suddenly vague, his words not forming properly as he stuttered about, talking in mumbling circles.

Lying. Thickskins did not have the mind for it. The hard sun clearly baked their brains as well as their exterior epidermis.

"There's a hinge, but ... I can't open it."

Kes stood there as HanNam went through the painful process of trying to prise open the trinket, brown stubby claws sliding uselessly over the smooth metal surface.

Gratefully, Kes saw a solution, and truth be told, anything would be better than watching the awkward creature attempt something that was clearly physically impossible. "Come with me, and bring that." Kes led him through the bazaar, ignoring surprised glances from rubbernecked onlookers and trying to take the route less travelled, leading him to Kes's private suite through the twists and turns. Once inside, Kes pointed to the analysis pad. HanNam placed the object down with gentle reverence.

"Don't tell anyone about this," Kes hissed, running a smooth hand over the display and beginning the diagnostic. Last thing he needed was someone reading meaning into his actions, especially now that the code had changed. He shivered, not wanting to think about the fate of a sibling who no longer held a lofty place in dome society. She chose the low way, spurning self-fertilisation for a messy interspecies exchange.

Kes looked down at the display, impatiently tapping manicured fingernails against metal. "You know that this doesn't mean I like you. I'm just curious to see what it is, that's all. Don't take this as an invitation to lance me."

"Is that all you softies think about?" HanNam had the good sense to look offended.

Kes resisted smirking, a difficult thing to do; a violent cheek twitch betrayed him. The codes of behaviour—he couldn't afford to make a mistake. Being alone with the revolting hominid was risky enough.

The display suddenly burst into life. The romantic images disturbed Kes. "It's called a locket," he said sourly, picking it up. There were meant to be pictures inside such trinkets. He opened it, but settled into disappointment at the sight of mere sand. Without thinking, he shoved it back into HanNam's hands.

"What did you just do?"

Kes turned swiftly to face the speaker. Pa-Ma looked from the display, then back to the locket lying in HanNam's hardened palm.

"Kes, a love gift, to one of them? Not you too!"

Kes spluttered in protest, but his Pa-Ma's eyes hardened. "You know the code. You've made your bed; now you have to lie in it." Kes released a shaky breath; strangely, he was heartened by the fact that HanNam looked as horrified as he felt.

Ami Hart (pseudonym for Jesse Colvin) is a writer, painter, thinker, gamer from "Quaky- town"—Christchurch, New Zealand. She dabbles in a multitude of genres, frequently complaining that she suffers MWD (multiple worlds disorder). She is currently writing her first science fiction novel. Ami blogs at http://www.amilibertyhartwriter.com and at http://liberty-jessie.blogspot.co.nz.

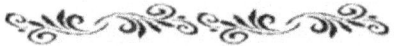

16. Sentience

Paula Friedman

All this happened before the Interstellar Manifest in Recognition of each world-born sentience.

We were still young. I was Parna's female cultural attaché on conquered Lanos, new to Erigan's soaring towers and the work. I loved the silvered skies, bold golden clouds, white waves. Garando was (surprisingly, as masculine Erigis there on Lanos are generally sombre like our own) a striking, gold-furred, brilliant creature, fluent in eight worlds' languages, communicator in each verbal, empath, warbler mode. Someone who had known and suffered much, my lithe and learned good friend and mentor in those months. So wondrous he was, Garando, as we trekked the blasted Flith peaks over Yomba, clambered rock shores to the ancient sculptures of the Isle of Lan, wandered torn museums where he helped me comprehend Erig traditions, and by evening leaned, sleek head to golden breast and toes to claws, together in the slow, bare rail-ride back to Erigan. I trembled beholding his dark warmth, longed to stroke soft fingertips along that tawny pelt, sense feathery feelers on my skin, his swift thoughts in my soul.

And he, self-trancing on my "innocence," yearned deep—I now know—too.

Remember, this was Parna-years before the Lanos Rising and resultant worlds-wide revolutions that, arising from the Seekers Movements of the 2460s, gave each sentience a sense of trusted self to freely seek out love. We were afraid.

"Hold me, beauty," Garando's tongue out-flicked. His fur misted my palms, his feelers coiled my arms. We rode the lift, gilt air below pricked by the darkened spires of Erigan. We wrapped together, heating, swarming dark electric. Squeezed at last into a narrow broken corridor, and lay upon his ivory warm-bed. Silver Moon glowed over Needle.

So few sentiences dared cross species then; I did not understand. He licked my eyelids; bathed in musk-scent, we sought new joy. Who could know a male Eregi needs, to reach a mode to merge a female ... what, ignorant, I could not give. For hours we squeezed, and yet, even adhering, lay unspent. Until, though shamed by my failure, I dared look up into his orbs.

And he said, "Ah well, beauty, I guess your longing for the alien arises only from some twist," and added, "I saw a healer once; you must, as well. That you may someday cease to twist an Erig's gift." Yet his feeler stroked my cheek.

I could not doubt him; I left, descending the Thousand Steps. His words had cut a horror of my heart.

Much as our invasion fleets had etched, through that whole millennium, horror into his world. Leaving the puppet caste and upper sex of Lanos to carve Erigis' minds. To teach them doubt of I and Thou, divide and isolate.

No matter. But it was only through Revolution's changes we could find our own free language and our truths of selves. Only in the years we struggled, together as one—we Parnese, Earthians, Sillas, Erigs—on Jaranda's barricades, space-trails of ancient Cortiex, darkest Har—could we learn, in sweat and tears, how deep all sentients love. Only then could I come, at last, to see Garando had been wrong, the "twisting" neither mine nor his but simply concepts foisted in Erigis by our long invasion and their loss, and in we Parnese females by our straitened lives.

I had only, wholly, longed for and loved him.

Now it is another courage needed, an age away on far Sil's sands, knowing what we briefly had and ever lost.

Paula Friedman is author of The Rescuer's Path (2012), which Ursula K. Le Guin has called "exciting, physically vivid, and romantic." Friedman has received two Pushcart nominations and several literary awards; her short fiction and poetry have appeared in numerous anthologies and magazines. She seeks a new siamese cat and a Macarthur, Nobel, or other major award/grant. Sentience appeared as a February 2014 Flash Fiction selection on Morgen Bailey's Writers Blog. friedman@gorge.net http://www.paula-friedman.com

17. Everyman Dies, But Not Everyman Lives

Mike Boggia

"Wonder what my friends would say?" Medic Chiron Zingaro's voice echoed from the cavern's obsidian walls. "I forgot. It doesn't matter to them. They're dead. Everybody's dead within twenty light years."

He laughed until he choked. They all died at once, together. I'm dying alone, without hope.

Dawn broke, day twenty after the crash. Zingaro struggled to his feet. Moving carefully on a makeshift crutch, he avoided stubbing the toes of his broken leg on the uneven floor. He paused at the entrance, leaned against the rough wall, and studied the foreboding, blood-red sunrise.

Silence unto the silence of deep space. A boulder studded landscape stretched before him. He limped across the charred terrain to the wreckage of the ship. I'll bring the last salvageable food here. After that ...

With the rising sun-star, the insidious wind stirred. A gentle, beguiling zephyr graduated to a stiff breeze and ended in the daily, moaning gale. He stared at the bronze cloud of hissing sand, wondering if the night's total silence was worse than the sibilant shh of sand. Cursing, he withdrew into the cavern, donned a respirator, and huddled on a pile of blankets.

Zingaro relived the last few heart-pounding minutes of disbelief and terror before the crash. He survived because he went into the linen closet to check supplies for sickbay. Three simultaneous explosions racked the craft. Bedding tumbled around him as he fell to the floor. Seconds later a shelf crushed his leg. Impact with the planet ripped the compromised airframe apart. Pain rendered Zingaro unconscious.

After he regained consciousness, the thought of survivors needing treatment, spurred him to drag himself into the wreckage. Discovering he was the only survivor was a depressing blow. Using a bent doorframe, he set and splinted the fracture, almost passing out several times.

Alone, with no chance of rescue and hampered by his injury, he calculated the odds of survival were zero.

The periphery of his vision caught movement at the entrance. He blinked, sat up, and rubbed his eyes. It's my imagination. Hell, no! Something's peering around a boulder.

"Damn!" Zingaro grabbed a chunk of jagged rock and prepared to defend himself.

Startled by his movement, it halted, just inside the opening.

What the devil? Appears to be a scabby, wart and horn-covered emaciated snake. He cocked his arm.

The creature froze for a moment. The horned, oval head moved in serpentine fashion.

"Get the hell out of here!" Zingaro flung the rock and missed his target.

The alien rolled into a ball, flipped over, belly exposed. Rudimentary appendages folded against the body.

Zingaro stared at it until curiosity prompted him to speak. "Okay, I'll let you stay."

The creature righted itself, crept deeper into the cavern, and curled up across from him, head resting on the mottled gray body. He guessed the beast fell asleep. A string of green tongue hung from a fringed, lipless mouth. Zingaro dozed and dreamed of another crash.

He was aboard a vessel, manned by creatures resembling the one that crawled into his place.

Frantic activity indicated a malfunction aboard ship. The craft stalled and began a steep descent toward the bronze planet. The crash, though not spectacular, killed or mortally injured the crew. One survived.

***

He shared his rations and named it Macabre. Macabre ate and drank miniscule amounts. Their food and water lasted two weeks.

Dehydration and starvation sucked fluid and flesh from Zingaro's body. Macabre sagged against him and dreamed.

"I'm dying, hopeless, but not alone," he rasped. He snuggled closer, embracing Macabre's skeletal body.

How did Macabre get to the entrance? I see four of him. He sank into darkness.

Zingaro awoke to the hum of a propulsion engine and saw Macabre curled up on a bench next to his. Macabre's thoughts entered his mind. You saved me. We return you to your kind.

He reached over and patted the warty body. "Thanks, pal. I wonder what Command will say about my 'first contact'?"

Mike Boggia's passion since childhood has been writing. He had a gothic novel, The Dungeon, written under the pen name Mary Lee Falcon, published in 1967, sold a short story to Mike Shane Mystery Magazine in 1973, and in 2013 had a short story in Mystic Tales from the Misty Swamp.

18. The Sound of Time

S.M. Kraftchak

Herbert knew those footsteps, he'd heard them before. Ba-lump, ba-lump, ba-lump, as steady as the tick-tock, tick-tock, tick-tock of the cuckoo's clock; first to the corner where ancient floorboards creak under leather boots that click and crack on gravel as they turn back to the middle of the room; ba-lump, ba-lump, ba-lump where steps shoosh sand and dirt between time-worn boards and then continue, ba-lump, ba-lump, wa-lum, wa-lum, wa-lum as his footsteps soften on the rug that hovers over the squishy dank darkness of the cellar where Herbert watches his precious gears turn, their teeth coming together, snick, snick, snick. They had done their job.

Squinting at the sand raining down in dirty veils, Herbert growls—low like a lion purring—deep in his throat at Adam. What now? What did he care about time? He hadn't spent a lifetime without the one he loved. Time was nothing to him but currency spent on banging his tankard down and roaring for another drink. To Herbert it meant days, standing by her headstone ... Elspeth L. George, beloved Daughter, died 1866 ... and nights fiddling in this dim basement. His clock had worked; now he had the time he needed.

After an hour of tick-tock, ba-lump footsteps; stomp and the man's roar, "Fine, I'm leaving."

"Finally," Herbert said, looking at his clock in the dim light.

Herbert's breath was ragged: puff-wheeze, puff-wheeze, puff-wheeze, but as steady as the scrip-plop, scrip-plop, scrip-plop of his feet and the tick-tock, tick-tock, tick-tock of a cuckoo's clock. He could make it. He had to. The wheels on the horse-drawn trolley rumbled as it gained speed on the next hill back. It would be here shortly. There she was.

"Adam, wait!" Elspeth whimpers as she pauses on the sidewalk, then steps into the street.

Puff-wheeze, puff-wheeze, puff-wheeze; he had to go faster; the whinnying and clattering ca-lump, ca-lump, ca-lump of a spooked horse and thundering wheels is growing louder. He couldn't let it happen again.

"Adam Wells, wait—" She stopped to tug at her boot heel caught in the tracks.

"Elspeth, I'm—puff-wheeze—coming!"

"Papa?"

Herbert reaches her as the trolley crests the hill. Ka-chang, ka-chang, ka-chang, the trolley bell warns; metal screeches on metal and the terrified horse squeals and thunders toward them.

"Move! Move! Move!" the conductor croaks, and waves.

Herbert thuds to his knees and pops the laces open on Elspeth's boot.

"Go-wheeze, go-wheeze, go-wheeze." Herbert shoves Elspeth as the runaway trolley bears down on them.

"Elspeth?" a man's voice cries out. "Elspeth, get out of there!" Adam roars and rushes back to the street as screaming and screeching metal meld in dissonance, smothering the sickening thud-thud, whuff.

"Papa? Papa? What were you thinking?" Elspeth says, with tears falling from her eyes onto her father's bloody shirt as she cradles him in her arms.

Herbert opens his eyes. Whuff-gurgle, whuff-gurgle, whuff and smiles. "I did it. I saved you. If he had left sooner, maybe—"

"But Mr. George, I was waiting to ask you for Elspeth's hand in marriage," Adam said.

"Yes, Papa, we're going to get married, because I'm pregnant."

Herbert looked between his daughter's face and Adam's face, his breath shallow with a soft tick, tick, tick as air just barely passed the pooling blood, and then smiled.

"When he's old enough, gurgle-wheeze, give my grandson a present from me, gurgle-wheeze, my clock and papers in the basement, gurgle-wheeze."

"No," Elspeth squawked. "We'll give him much more. We'll give him your name."

Herbert smiled, "I'd like that, click, but don't saddle him, click, with a name the kids, click, will make fun of, wheeze. Call him H.G." Herbert's eyes closed, his breath a long low wheeze, gurgle, gurgle, tock.

Elspeth fought back tears as she watched her father fade. "Herbert George Wells, I like that name."

S. M. Kraftchak notes: As a writer who spends most of her time in other worlds with dragons, elves, and the occasional alien, S.M. still enjoys sunrise on the beach, sunset in the mountains, and portraying Elizabeth Tudor. She has two dogs, who think they are footrests, a cat who thinks she's a blanket, and three awesome daughters. Her husband is her best friend, her harshest critic, and her most fervent supporter. Writing is S.M.'s passion.

19. Escape from Amoluz

Helmuth Kump

The red sun of this wretched planet, Amoluz, burned the soil around Pytor with brutal efficiency.

From his partial shade in the ragged mangrove-like growth, he tried to forget about the Raakei's advance. It was done. He now yearned only to reach out to Ruth.

The Raakei had disrupted all dimensional communications. A simplex digital radio was Pytor's only backup. He'd have to cope with the time required for a text conversation: six minutes for the signal to reach Ruth at the outpost, and six more for her reply. It was all he had, but it worked.

"The enemy's latest attack caught me by surprise. I'm trying to shield myself until it's cool enough to return to the shuttle. How do you like the new facility there? I can't believe we were together a week ago. I miss you."

Pytor hit "send" and peered up through the branches at the antenna, which he'd set up in the highest mangrove he could reach. The indicator on the antenna's base glowed green, signifying a successful uplink.

While waiting for a reply, he looked to his left at the yellow-tinged waves of acidic ocean, breaking on the shore about 200 meters away. The constant roar brought him back to summers past, when his father took him and his brother Adam fishing in Captree Park. Memories of plump flounder, pale sand, and golden sun filled his tired mind. His father and brother were gone now, victims of the enemy's chemical poisoning that devastated New York. Pytor had no inclination to return after that.

The buzz of the transceiver broke his reminiscing. His heart jumped as he saw Ruth's reply.

"I miss you so much, Pytor. This is a huge campus. In one of the halls here there is a keyboard, the heavy mechanical kind. It says Steinway, does this mean anything? I put my hands on the keys and imagine your hands on top of mine, teaching me."

He imagined her loving embrace. His fingers typed quickly. "Yes, Steinway pianos were highly prized. The factory was near our home in Astoria. Feel my hand on yours, guiding your fingers into place. Then we push down together, sounding a full major chord."

Their exchange was the only thing keeping Pytor from going mad in this brutal furnace. He tried to cover any exposed flesh, but it was impossible to block every inch. Whenever he felt the blisters start, he'd shift any way he could to move that area into the shade, but that would of course expose another area of skin.

He heard another buzz. Was this another message from Ruth? No, page after page of garbled characters were filling the display.

It was then Pytor noticed the approaching cloud bank. The red sun abruptly disappeared behind the thick cumulus layer racing across the sky, and twilight replaced the red sunlight. Cursing the unstable weather of Amoluz, he left his mangrove refuge and started running toward the shuttle, leaving his gear behind. He could see his breath as he tried to stay warm by running faster. A few gray acidic snowflakes swirled around him. His lungs burned.

The leading edge of the pulse caught up with him from behind. He left his feet as the shock wave hurled him forward ten meters. The rocky soil scraped his forehead and cheek open as he landed.

Dazed, Pytor got up again, feeling the residual thrust at his back. It pushed him onward, as if he were running downhill. He felt blood trickle out and freeze on his cheeks and chin. Gratefully, the shape of his spacecraft was now discernible a few hundred meters ahead.

Inside the transition room, Pytor looked at his body. Bright red blisters on his legs, arms, and neck contrasted with bluish frost nip on his toes and fingertips. His scraped-up face would take a while to heal. But, for now, he was okay.

Using an onboard transceiver in simplex mode he sent another message to Ruth. "Made it back to the shuttle. Are your hands on the Steinway?"

Twelve long minutes later came her reply. "Yes, they are, waiting for yours."

An information technology professional residing in Crafton, Pennsylvania, Helmuth Kump has had two short stories published and is presently germinating a science fiction novel. When not working or writing, the native of Queens, New York, enjoys running, playing drums, chess, opera, amateur radio, casino blackjack, books on metaphysics, and spending time with his two adult sons.

20. Connections

Amos Parker

"**G**o on."

On one knee in the alien soil, Jasper pointed at the plant's radial red tendrils. Cassie, with a glance up at the high galaxy of nighttime stars, shook her head. In the low Delanine gravity, her blonde tresses flew windless and wild.

"No. No, Jas. I can't."

Her wide blue eyes locked with Jasper's browns. His hair hung cut to a small fraction of the length of hers, matching his eyes. He looked up at the stars, as she had. The thin Delanine atmosphere scattered a star field twice Earth's midnight density.

"It won't hurt, Cas. That I can promise. Not like the past."

Both of them wore the same loose green clothes they'd come out of the long hypersleep wearing.

"It can't be love then, now can it Jas."

Off in the distance, at the base of a craggy hill, the ship Valentine vented steam from thrusters. None of the others there had changed either.

Her fingers were long, white and delicate. His were short, brown and clumsy. His palm alone had a red tendril piercing its lifeline. Close to fifty sprouted from the blue, bud-like pod a stone's throw away. And, in that gravity, it was a muscular throw.

Soft voices called from the ship and echoed off a cliff near Jasper and Cassie. Somewhere, water gurgled. The tendril pulsed and glowed.

It had taken Jasper some time to calm Cassie down. No wonder.

"I'm going back now, Jas. Please pull that off and come with me. I don't trust the scouting reports the way you do."

"I never told you how much I love you, Cas."

"What?"

The young woman stood up and then took a step away. In the bright starlight, she could see the acne pits on the older man's face. He said nothing.

"No. You never told me. For –"

She twitched.

"For how long haven't you been telling?"

"Since the first tests they ran on us, back on Earth. Rorschach. Newton. Shakespeare. In the Hive."

"Even then?"

"Too scared to say so until ..."

Jasper closed his four fingertips and one thumbtip on their palm-penetrating scarlet vine. It hid the biting tip from her blue sight. As if his gentle touch impeded it, the shoot bulged beyond his fingerprints.

"Until now. They were right, you know."

Still a step further away, Cassie knelt.

"What's it feel like, Jas?"

He smiled. She could see it was different. Before, he'd seemed half dead. Now, he seemed to throb, like the penetrating tendril. Something underground made the air vibrate. And the air smelled of ... cinnamon.

"First I'll talk about before. Before I felt empty. All my life I felt it, like I was cut off from the flow of life in living people. We're all in our own little vacuums, you know? Humans talk, so, like my mother said, we lost our ability to read minds."

"Funny. My mother said the same thing."

"Now, Cas, I feel ... half full."

"Not half empty?"

"I know. Everyone took me as a pessimist, before. I was, of course. No wonder. But now fullness is right here. The bond. Full-blooded unity. I'm looking at it."

He smiled at her. The warmth of it struck under her ribs.

"I'm looking at her, Cas."

He pointed at the vine again.

"So go on."

She trembled, tickled by something.

"Make us whole?"

"You feel empty, don't you?"

She hesitated, for a very long moment, and at last nodded.

"Always. I ... always thought marriage would make me whole, at last when it came. My stiff father said that."

Jasper laughed. A band of lighter brown scarred the skin at the base of his left ring finger, mere centimeters from the tendril's bite.

"Go on, Cas."

Her sigh at that came out as deep as the star field. Then she nodded. She laid her left hand, palm up, beside the red cord. That stone's throw off, the pod bloomed.

The tendril wriggled, tip rising, and dove home.

Amos Parker is a starving writer, graduate of the University of Vermont, and resident of the United State of Vermont. He knows his muse is bereft of protein, fat, vitamins, and minerals. And so, he does not cannibalize her.

EDGES

21. Summer Bites

J.F. Williams

It was only a few miles beyond the Foggy Oaks exit, then a right turn onto county route 3. Another few miles before he caught the crude wooden sign in his headlights. He turned onto the dirt road just ahead of it. Jesus, I'm late, he thought. Katy's going to kill me

The cabin was hidden by tree cover as he pulled the car up, but Martin could see the porch bathed in the amber light of a "bug bulb." Down from the porch, the land fell steeply to the edge of the lake, and he could just now see the full moon's reflection, like a row of silvery worms floating on the lake's surface.

Katy was sitting at a rough-hewn wooden table on the porch. "Finally," she said. "Are you all done?"

"Yeah. For two weeks. Where are the boys?" He pulled up a chair, bent down for a kiss, and laid out the evening paper on the table. She didn't seem too upset, he thought.

"The boys are already in bed. Can you believe it?" she smiled and pulled a sweater around her shoulders. It was a cool evening for July. "They're exhausted. I'm exhausted from watching them! They went swimming all day. I just stayed down there to watch. They were good. They didn't even go near the buoys."

"Tired them out, eh. Good."

"It wasn't just that. The mosquitoes. They were eating them alive when they got out. Big fat ones. I killed a bunch."

"Eww. That must've been bloody."

"Huh? No. There was no blood. I checked for bites and Tommy had a big one on the back of his neck." She patted a spot at the base of her skull. "He was crying and digging at it. I used that cream, and I gave them a Benadryl."

"Oh." Martin was focused on the paper now and was starting to read the front page when he heard a buzzing. It grew louder and stopped, followed by the faintest humming. He noticed a bulbous mosquito crawling slowly along the far edge of the table. He folded his paper and slammed it fast as he could. "Good one!" shouted Katy.

When Martin lifted the paper, he saw a mess. Pieces of wing and leg and thorax were scattered across the headline: "NEW REVELATIONS ON LEAKER'S BACKGROUND." He pulled off as much of the remains as he could, but it was viscous and sticky, though colorless. At least there wasn't blood.

"This pisses me off," he said, pointing at the headline. "They already convicted this guy in the press. I don't know if he's a good guy or a bad guy, but it looks like the press guys already decided and that makes me suspicious. And why's the government after him if the secrets, the stuff he leaked, aren't real?"

"I hear ya," she answered. "I don't trust the government not to do this stuff. I don't care which government. What's to stop them? The stuff about the micro drones spying on us. That's scary stuff. Why would that guy make it up?"

"I dunno." He shook his head. "Whatever they say about him, I think what he said is for real. I'm certainly not feeling any safer. Anything to eat?"

Tommy crouched inside the cabin, just under the screen window, stone-faced, taking it all in. He was getting mad. He didn't know why, but what his mom and dad said was making him mad. "Government" and "secrets" were making him mad, and "leak" made him repress a growl. He wanted to make them stop that talking but he held back. He felt the tension of it; his hands clenched air, his arms and thighs trembled with the urge to pounce. But he held back. Minutes passed, and his parents continued to speak. He remained still, sometimes absentmindedly touching the tiny, hair-like structure that rose exactly five millimeters from the spot where the mosquito bit him. But mostly, he just listened, and tried to keep himself from killing them, because he knew he should be listening now.

J.F. Williams has been working in Information Technology for the past quarter-century but started out as a proofreader and spent years writing synopses of movies and TV programs for newspaper TV listings, placing him among the most widely read anonymous writers in the U.S. and Canada of that time. He published his first novel, an epic science-fiction adventure called The Brickweavers, in August 2012.

22. Boyhood's End

Andy McKell

They moved into the new house in the midsummer heat, when the lake mirrored the sky's longing for the breath of a breeze and the forest trees hung their heads in exhaustion. Bobby thought it the most wonderful summer ever, and when it came to a close, he would become twelve—the perfect age! He just wished and wished for his last, lingering baby tooth to fall before he started his new school.

The creatures of the lakeland forest filled the air with sound—buzzing, cricketing, chirruping, wailing, hooting. He heard foxes coughing, distant deer barking, badgers snuffling close to the house, and other, unknown things scuffling the parchment-dry leaves underfoot or uttering their own calls, challenges, and complaints. It was a sweet relief after the horrid, inconsiderate, machine-driven noise of the city.

He bravely explored his new territory. He heard soft rustlings, spotted tiny movements .... But he was twelve—almost. He was unafraid. He had grown out of magic and monsters, except for that last, lingering affection for the tooth-fairy, that sweet, gentle spirit who loves children. Yes, the tooth fairy loved children.

He sought secret paths and places; waterfalls and pools; slippery, moss-covered rocks. He sought dark caves to explore with the brave gang he would recruit.

So it was in the woods that he fell, bashed his face, and ripped loose that last, lingering baby tooth and watched as the precious token skittered away. Ignoring his bleeding knee and ripped pants, he scrabbled in the dirt for his trophy. And there it was; but alongside it, another thing, a bigger thing, a handfilling thing; a second tooth, a huge tooth, a giant's tooth, a monster's tooth, yellowed and curved, wickedly pointed; a tooth for ripping and tearing flesh. He grabbed both teeth, hugged them to his chest. Joyously, he raced and stumbled home, ignoring the risk of another fall, caring not a jot.

Mom celebrated with him this symbol of a boyhood's ending, and admired his find. She grinned when he begged for an early night, to give the tooth fairy enough time to handle the double donation. Mom kissed him goodnight and gave him a special hug.

Of course, Bobby couldn't sleep. He could feel the curve of the monster tooth through his pillow. Excitement prodded him to toss and to turn. Excitement made his thoughts churn, made him wonder if the "people" tooth fairy could handle this load, or if the owner had its own tooth fairy; and if so, what the tooth fairy for such a monster would be like. Excitement finally exhausted him, drained him, overfilled his swirling thoughts until his brain closed down and the sleep required by the magical exchange of tooth and coin overtook him.

Until midnight.

The noise came to him through his sleep. It was not a natural sound, not a scuffling or a barking or a hooting or a chirruping. It was a thud-thud-thud, it was a roar, it was a splintering of trees. Worst of all, it was approaching, and approaching fast.

Bobby screamed and leaped from his bed, sweating, trembling. Noise, stench and heat—not of these human lands—embraced, enveloped, engulfed him. Light filled his room, a bright, horrid, sickly-green light; a light that wrapped around his body, rendering him as immobile as if in the grip of vast, powerful jaws.

His entire being was gripped, shaken, and examined to its very core. He felt his body twisting, turning, turning.

And with the monster's tooth fairy came boyhood's end.

Andy McKell is a new writer of speculative fiction, whose short stories are starting to appear in various anthologies. He retired early from the IT world and enjoys acting when he gets the chance. Married with three daughters, all pursuing careers in the visual arts, he currently lives in Luxembourg, Europe. andy@andymckell.com http://www.andymckell.com

23. Sting

Marianne G. Petrino

The droning rulers of summer hibernated. Carried by a light breeze, snowflakes silently drifted across a moonlit, barren field and covered the burrows that gave the enemy refuge from the cold. Summer meant resurrection for the aliens, whose renewed hunger would cull humanity once more in the continuation of their life cycle.

Miranda rubbed the returning frost from the window with her frayed sleeve. Although hidden by the grey night, the glittering stars of Orion still shone, the symbol of the Women Who Hunted, upon a diminished Earth. In a broken-down garage in what used to be Ishpeming, one of the sticky traps had finally captured a specimen, bringing hope to her drafty cabin.

The fretful chirp of a battered timer drew her attention to the plastic bottles that gently rotated over pots of boiling water. Duct tape and chicken-wire science now helped secure the possibility of a future. She removed the makeshift spit and studied the cloudy contents. Preparing the injections was an easy task; choosing the vector children would earn her hatred and praise.

Miranda moved the spit to a wall rack. "Taffy and a corn dog." She tapped a container that held death, a heartbeat to the lost past. "What I wouldn't give...." But the pleasures of those easy summers had gone extinct.

Years back, scientists had worried about the growing numbers of mosquitoes that had carried unprecedented viral threats. Research into insect control had jumped, but the miasma of politics, and the bickering that shaped it, had kept funding limited. Money, and the biological discoveries it bought, could have helped them gain an edge in the beginning of the invasion.

The absurd stories of alien visitors to the Earth had been true all along. And with a tiny hitchhiker, evolution had taken an unexpected leap in an interstellar nursery.

The returning invaders inside the armada of one-way-only spaceships were an outwardly distressing twin to the buzzing, biting terrestrial insects, but man-sized. In the tropical regions, the swiftly reproducing spacesquitoes had eaten themselves out of prey and had died. Like an unexpected ending, only the cooling days of autumn in the temperate regions and the ultimate frost of winter had saved what was left of pest-shocked mankind. The remaining aliens had retreated deep underground, for they and their progeny were equally victims of their own biology. Yet their limitation gave their food source time to multiply.

A gust rattled the window pane. Miranda shivered. The fattened children, juicy with virus-plagued blood, drugged and scattered like seeds in a field, would feed the gluttonous emerging females during the spring lust. But all of their newly fertilized eggs would rot under the biological assault she had created.

A clock chimed softly four times. She reached for a kettle to keep a ritual to prop up her sanity. The Women Who Hunted had provided the specimen for her to study and manipulate, but the game may have always been lost.

One nagging doubt made it all seem futile and added to the insomnia born of the sacrifices she must commit: What if these were engineered beings created by a superior race to scour a world clean? These spacequitoes exceeded the spiracle-bound limitations of any insect found on Earth, through morphological mutations too precise for nature. But their victories over mankind came from their numbers, not their intelligence. If her hypothesis were true, why hadn't their masters already come to finish the cleansing of Earth?

A bit of blue poked out of the snow. Could this be the crocus of a final spring?

Miranda sipped her tea.

Marianne G. Petrino (aka Marianne G. Petrino-Schaad) was born in the Bronx, NY, in 1955, and that single fact has shaped her entire life. She has survived too many professions to count. She currently resides in Arlington, VA, with her husband and her cat, and enjoys a freelance lifestyle writing novels and pursuing voice acting. ninetiger@aol.com http://www.ninetiger.net

24. Moments to Remember

W.A. Fix

It was one of those moments that imprints into the collective memory of an entire family. Everything was perfect. A full moon reflecting on the lake, clouds floating like puffs of smoke on a light breeze, and there were so many stars one truly felt the awesome vastness of space. The mountain air was crisp and held a chill that the campfire offset. The four sat around the fire in silence enjoying the warmth that came from the moment, more than the fire. Wayne poked at the coals with a green sapling that he had used earlier to cook his hot dogs. Without warning, another sapling invaded his space and pushed his away from the fire. He looked up to see Kathy, his thirteen-year-old daughter, smiling and ready to dual for ownership of his spot in the coals.

"You little creep, that's my spot," said Wayne.

She pointed the flaming tip of her sapling at him and said, "On guard." As she squinted and set her jaw with determination, they touched swords briefly, chuckled, and then went back to tending their own section of the flames.

"Mom, can I have a Coke?" said Billy

"No, honey, it's too close to bedtime," said Jennifer. When she saw the frown on his face, she added, "Sweetie, that's too much caffeine and sugar, this late. If you're thirsty, there is plenty of bottled water."

"Knock, knock…, hello! I'm sorry to bother you folks." The woman entered the campsite from the dense forest that surrounded them. "I'm so sorry, but I got separated from my friends and it started getting cold. Do you mind if I just warm up?" She walked up to the fire and extended her hands, palms out, over the flames.

Surprised by the intrusion, Wayne stood. "Where on earth did you come from?" he said to her. "Billy, get a blanket." The woman was slender and middle-aged and wore hiking boots, blue jeans, and a light sweater. "How long have you been out there?" he said. Billy arrived with a blanket, and Wayne draped it across her shoulders. "Are you hungry?"

"Thank you, I'm just fine," she said. She extracted a phone from her back pocket and began dialing.

Wayne smiled and said, "That won't do you any good up here. There's no phone service for at least fifty miles."

"Yes, I know," she said, pushed a final button, smiled and met his eyes for the first time. "It isn't a phone."

The campsite was instantly flooded with bright white light. Wayne felt euphoric and a tingling swept over him. He was transfixed by the woman's black eyes and, in them, he could see the countless years of her existence. He heard whimpering and knew it was Jennifer. A piercing scream sent chills through him but he couldn't tell who it was. "Mommy, help me mommy"—that was Billy. Wayne tried to move and could do nothing. He felt pain in his abdomen, yet somehow it didn't hurt. Another scream and he still could do nothing. He began to cry, tears welling in his eyes, streaming over his cheeks and into his ears. When did he lie down? Then Kathy yelled, "Daddy!" There was another scream, but this time it was his.

It was one of those moments that imprints into the collective memory of an entire family. Something was wrong. The moon had set. The fire had burned down and now cast a sinister light on the scene. He held the smoking sapling that was inexplicably only a foot long.

"Mommy, I don't feel good," said Billy.

"I know, sweetheart. Let's go to bed. Maybe you'll feel better in the morning," said Jennifer.

Wayne watched the vacant eyes of his daughter and saw consciousness slowly returning. Kathy glanced around confused, then met his gaze and he saw darkness in her that had never been there before.

W. A. Fix (a.k.a. Bill Fix) is a retired information technology manager, who lives with his wife and three cats in the suburbs of San Diego, California. He has "toyed" with writing all his life and recently became more serious about the craft. Other interests include photography and golf.

25. Becoming Again

J.J. Alleson

"So ... we right direction." Jerala's statement was more accusation than question. The accused watched him with eyes like black ice. The other three circled them, still a loose-knit group after six days in close company. The women were Nye and Kismet. The men: Jerala, Thomas, and Olain.

In the murderous fahrenheit of an endless summer, it was Kismet who stood toe to toe, if not eye to eye, with Jerala. Nye stepped in, cooing mediation. "Please. Our quest is almost over."

They were five strangers whose paths had crossed on the way to Syti, the place where Earth's population converged as one corporate laboratory. Four had left behind the braying scorn of their people.

One had left a pile of unbleached bones.

"You all sure? We close?" Jerala was a pedantic nit-picker; an outcast who had offended bio-engineers with no time for clinical validations. As they travelled, he spoke of better days three hundred years ago.

"Big fuss 'bout oil once. 'Til one company found ways to make hydrocarbons. Used corn starch, sugar cane ... even grasses. All happy-happy. Couldn't save 'zone layer, though. We overheated. The UVs came. Rogues took over. Stole those catalytic conversion techniques and put melanin in the mix for the staying-alive market. Not like the polka-dots from chemo, but all over smooth-smooth."

They all knew the history. The black-body scramble had, overnight, turned pariah-paupers into the Untouchable Dalit Gods of Afrik-Syti, protected day and night from contact with desperadoes seeking skin-scrapes. When wealthy clients demanded more customised physiques, biochemists had simply added another transhuman DNA string. The procedure, a powerful injection known as "The Mosquito", was aggressively promoted. Until a glitch began to throw up terrifying foetal deformities.

"Mosquito wiped out billions. Made billionaires. Many more in Syti, waiting to become."

But not everyone cared for Jerala's protocols. In a private moment, the ultra-slender Olain expressed concerns. "He's completely paranoid."

"Should we eat him?" Twelve-year-old Thomas had been alone a year. Like many facing starvation, he had learned pragmatism at the dinner table.

Kismet winked her agreement. "Why not?"

Nye's dark eyes flashed angrily at Kismet's shark-like instinct for the kill. "We can't eat Jerala. We need his stronger moral discipline."

But her words fell away into empty air.

***

Early dawn, the group awoke, ate, and left camp. Already Kismet's moonlit glow was shifting towards its midday onyx. Aquamarine hair fell towards child-bearing hips, cloaking breasts from which no infant could ever safely suckle.

At six-foot-five, with a land-and-water speed that blurred the vision, Kismet embodied that supreme throw of the DNA dice. A playful fate had granted her, at conception, an almost perfect Mosquito. Her glance at the discarded hump of fur was simply practical. "Should we bury it?"

"For the love of Dalit, Kismet! It's him!" Beneath Olain's hissed anger lay a good deal of satiated guilt.

"Didn't you enjoy ... him, Olain?" Kismet watched Olain, her eyes speculating something that no one there could decipher. Or wanted to.

Thomas jumped in quickly. "He was delicious." Thomas's limbs were equally useful for killing, eating, or running. He would apply all six, he decided, if Kismet ever came for him. Easing closer to Nye, he asked, "Do you think we'll become human again? In Syti?"

Nye smiled reassuringly. "Of course. They have a faster, stronger Mosquito now." All ethics had been left behind with Jerala's carcass. But Nye could still honour his memory. Turning to Kismet, she asked, "How you know right direction?"

Kismet gave her an open-mouthed grin. And each companion silently counted the endless, endless rows of teeth.

"Smell blood."

Thomas fought down the urge to seek shelter under Nye. He wished that her great wings held the power of flight. Then she could carry Olain and himself, coiled on her back, safely to Syti. Or to anywhere that would be far, far away from Kismet.

J.J. Alleson is a London-based freelance editor, multi-genre writer, and poet. She writes across the spectrum of romance, science fiction, murder mystery, and the paranormal. Her anthology of science fiction short stories, A Step in Time, will be available on Amazon, Smashwords, and other online platforms from December 2014. jjalleson@yahoo.com http://www.jjalleson.com

26. Unnatural Gas

Thaddeus Howze

An industrialist put on his plastic face, his expensive suit, and dragged an indentured lawyer into town with him. His Bentley arrived in a cloud of choking dust and stinging flies.

The town had gathered around a podium to listen to the complaints of some locals while they waited for the industrialist to arrive.

He took the podium, confident, smiling but after a few minutes, one of the townsfolk hurled something which landed with a solid thunk on the raised wooden stage. It was an old Colt revolver. Already loaded.

The industrialist looked closer at the crowd. He noted their pale mien. Many were coughing into towels. The bitter iron stink of blood wafted through the air. He knew that scent, intimately. Their condition had to do with residue from the hydraulic fracturing process.

He considered their condition ... unfortunate.

His gaze swept over the crowd but he appeared unaffected. "What's this for?" he asked as he gingerly picked up the gun.

"If you plan on robbing people you should be appropriately armed," someone shouted from a distance.

"I don't understand what you mean. I'm genuinely happy to report how wealthy we're becoming through your sacrifice. It's legal, I assure you." Unlike the industrialist, the attorney refused to meet anyone's eyes.

Looking around, the industrialist saw the stage stood in a pool of stagnant and foul-smelling water. "You should do something about your plumbing." It was then he noticed the stones people carried.

Reverend Ames staggered up to the front of the crowd, his eyes rheumy, but still sharp enough to see their way through to the heart of a man. "We are a god-fearing people. Galatians, chapter 6 verse 7: Be not deceived; God is not mocked: for whatsoever a man soweth, that shall he also reap."

The reverend spit and threw his stone at the industrialist and his lawyer. Others followed suit. Ducking, the two men tried to escape but large unhappy townsfolk waited at the foot of the ladder with metal bats.

The industrialist pointed the gun at the crowd. "Don't make me use this." A rain of stones arced through the air with more hitting than missing. The lawyer dropped and lay still. Shaken the industrialist fired the weapon at the Reverend.

The weapon flared and in seconds, vapors beneath the podium ignited, with the contaminated water beneath the stage acting as fuel. Both men were surrounded and engulfed by a makeshift funeral pyre.

No one fled.

The townsfolk leaned forward, silently savoring the screams of the two men. One or two looked a touch uncomfortable, but no one turned their back to the flames.

The reverend smiled at his parishioner who had given the industrialist the gun filled with flaring blanks. He turned his gaze toward the fire and with venom said, "Yes, sir. You are so right. We should do something about those leaky water pipes. Not to worry, the water stops burning in a couple of hours. Plenty of time for you to get used to your new accommodations in Hell."

The townsfolk rejoiced quietly and agreed to never speak of this.

When the methane was expended, only a pile of dark ash remained of the stage, the industrialist, and his counsel. As the townspeople turned, the pile of ash shifted suddenly and slowly the industrialist stood up and brushed the ash that used to be a podium, and possibly a lawyer, off of his once again pristine suit.

The townspeople stood agape. Dust rose from his footsteps as he walked from the ashes toward his car. He turned, the setting sun behind him.

"Just who did you people think you were getting in bed with?" His horns and winged shadow lingered in the setting sunlight, reaching out toward the townsfolk for an instant, as he got into his car.

I can't believe they did that. People can still surprise me.... The roar of his Bentley could be heard over the sounds of water mains and wells exploding, fire flowing toward the very center of town. No street was clear, no avenues for escape; a river of flame from every direction.

Collectively, they screamed, cowered, and burned.

Nearby, a murder of crows took wing and celebrated.

Thaddeus Howze is a technology consultant, science enthusiast, and speculative fiction author. His short fiction collection, Hayward's Reach, *came out in 2011. His writings revolve around environmental themes and question the nature and value of humanity in a world enamored of technological cleverness. See his speculative fiction at* http://hubcityblues.com.

CONFRONTATIONS

27. Time of the Phoenix

Carrol Fix

I was the first to make contact. I awoke from my dreaming slumber to hear the screeching collapse of my distant siblings. Fear gripped me and slowed my folding processes, making my leaves tremble as I drew them inward to protect them within my firm bark fiber. I could almost feel my sap congeal in terror, as I began the process of bending my denuded boughs downward against my trunk. As I waited, the sounds of death continued. Reluctantly, I began withdrawing my roots from the nourishing soil, pulling them upward into my root hand, while disengaging my working hand from the side of my trunk. When five walking branches remained, I bent my trunk, resting the limbs firmly on the ground. I straightened my other half, drawing my root arm down, with my "face," as the humans call it, near the top in the position we use when migrating and meeting others of our kind.

Humans came to our planet in the year 9, when we were fully arisen, and they found our world lush and promising. They began clearing space for their settlements, and thousands of my family perished before I managed to communicate our intelligence. Our process of Inversion takes nearly an hour to complete; one of them could cut down six of us before we could walk among them. They say we look like birch trees and that, once killed, our bodies function in the same manner as their wood.

I managed to make the humans understand me, even though our sounds were nothing alike in the beginning. They ceased murdering us and eventually we could speak together. I learned their language, and a few of my siblings also were willing to make the effort. For many years, we maintained an uneasy coexistence. More and more humans arrived, and our own population increased, causing conflicts over choice land—where the humans invariably prevailed.

By the year 58, there were open disputes; the humans found minerals they considered valuable, but which were life-sustaining elements for us. The inevitable happened and, despite some protests from the original humans, new arrivals began killing us to clear the land they wanted to exploit. They built structures from our bodies, burned us for fuel, and drove us from our rich food sources.

Lacking the mineral nourishment they needed, my brothers and sisters living closest to human settlements began deteriorating; losing rational thought processes. In year 89, a large group of my nearly wild siblings attacked a human colony, inflicting deadly devastation upon their tormentors. Because human lives were lost, the resultant backlash saw hundreds of thousands of us destroyed. We lost our homes to the invaders, who continued to pillage our planet to satisfy their greed, slaying us without mercy. For the next ten years, we gradually fled to the barren slopes of the mountains, eking out a miserly existence.

As always, we began our celebration in the year 99. Only a hundred thousand of us remained, but we gleaned enough sheddings of leaves and unwanted branches to light the ritual fires. Each night, we watched our tiny line of dancing flames, while our grandmothers told stories of the Times Before. New sprouts of This Time listened raptly. We all waited in anticipation.

This is the year 100 and it has begun, as it has since the dawn of time. At first the ground trembles. Plumes of smoke and steam from the mountaintops waft softly against the blue sky. Across our planet, the volcanoes awaken from their 100-year sleep. For 1000 days, the mountains will pour forth rivers of flaming lava. They will cause the ground to shudder and shake and to break open vast chasms that will devour the humans. Before the volcanoes return to their century-long rest, their mighty wrath will cleanse our planet of the alien infestation.

The conflagration will consume us and protect us, and the volcanoes' blessings will replenish our food sources from the belly of our planet. In time, my family and I will rise from beneath the ashes, and reclaim our home. When, in our eternal cycle, we arise again, and again, we will tell of this Time Before and vow that our world always will belong only to us.

Carrol Fix is a short-story writer and novelist whose science fiction work includes the novel Mishka: Book One of the Quadrate Mind. She is currently writing the second book in the Quadrate Mind series, while working on a young-adult fantasy novel, Worlds Apart. "Time of the Phoenix" appeared in the May, 2013 issue of Perihelion Science Fiction.
CarrolFix@LillicatPublishers.com http://www.mishkabook.com

28. Meek Survive

Richard Bunning

No one really knows how long Treen have lived on the Earth: literally, sub-terra, under the feet of humans. They, themselves, claim to have almost always been there, though it is hard to find many traces of them in the historical records, between the writing of the Book of Revelations and the treasured Eagle papers of the 1950s. However, Venus is so close that it is hard to believe that they didn't at least regularly visit.

The Current Meekon of the Treen, Ampson Meek, had greatly expanded Treen bases on Earth. As humans had emigrated, they had steadily been replaced by Treen settlers, who have no trouble dealing with the oxygen-depleted atmosphere. Most humans had left for less overexploited planets centuries ago, but ties had never been completely broken. There had been a state of peaceful coexistence between all but a few renegade Meeks and humans since the death of "The Supreme Scientist, Chairman Mekong" in the 1990s.

***

We imagine ourselves looking back through history into the last human military outpost, entrenched deep in the Underground tunnels of the once City of London, the Waterloo Brigade. In these final days of mankind's tenure of the Earth, the troops are being led by General Don Read. He has a deeply ingrained hatred of Treen and is determined to make sure the Meek never inherit the Earth.

By then, most humans have long accepted that prophesies in the old scriptures would be fulfilled. The Governors of Gliese were only too pleased at the prospect of being able to rid the exchequer of the expense of running the last Earth Unit. Read knows that departure is inevitable. However, if he can help it, this won't be before he has seen the Treens "burn in Hell". Reed is intent on making the Earth uninhabitable, even for the hardy Versuvians, before man departs.

***

"I will turn the surface of the Earth into the fires of Hell. I'll watch the bloody Meeks burn. How can I convince the fleet to launch a full atomic strike against the Meekon? I need to make out that we come under attack as we dismantle our defences prior to withdrawal. Those I trust least, Dare's second division, will be my pawns. No other units ever question my orders. That bloody Meekon-loving Colonel Daniel Dare, how fitting to destroy him with his alien friends.

***

"Launch a drone strike on Bedford, wide pattern, atomic warheads. Fire on my command!"

"But sir, isn't that where Dare's unit are?"

"They have been overwhelmed in a Treen attack, led by the Meekon himself, who intends to keep humans to breed as slaves. We will also be overrun before the Evacuation Force arrives, unless we strike whilst we are sure to catch the Treen leadership off-guard. I have received a dispatch telling me that Dare himself is already dead. We must act now, burning them and all the Earth."

"Sir, I refuse to carry out such an order."

"Launch, damn it. How dare you disobey a direct command, Lieutenant Dolos."

"I have higher orders, sir. In fact, you are under arrest. You see, the Quads never left barracks. You have been fooled into believing that your earlier orders were carried out. Colonel Dare is still right here. We all knew that your hatred runs so deeply that you would try to destroy the Treen at any cost. We are at peace with the Meekon, as you well know. They are even assisting our safe evacuation. The Governors now have reason to be done with you."

"This is insubordination. I command you to fire. You are deceived if you think you can defy me. We will leave nothing but a burning desert for the little Meek bastards."

"It is not we who are deceived. Chekov, show Mister Read to his quarters. As from this morning, General Dare is in command. We simply preferred you to condemn yourself before we acted. It is General Dare's personal wish that you be slung into Mount Etna, right down into the fires of hell. A bastard that would see his own troops murdered to deceive mankind into unleashing a holocaust on other peace-loving sentient beings deserves no less a funeral pyre."

[Story inspired by the original Eagle comic, 1950–1969, UK]

Richard Bunning is an author of speculative fiction. He has also published reworked neoclassical plays, a totally daft gift book, and short stories in a mix of genres. His best-known book to date is Another Space in Time. His website, geared towards the support of independent authors across many genres, is http://richardbunningbooksandreviews.weebly.com. richard.lw.bunning@gmail.com

29. The Horde

Tom Tinney

It was five hundred years ago, when the Horde had arrived. It was an early spring, before the crops had even sprouted. That is how the story goes.

They were here twenty seasons. That is all the time they needed to strip the Earth bare, lay waste to the great cities and scatter the survivors.

They came from the heavens.

They did not speak or announce their intent to the people, nor ask their permission; they just began mining.

They did not attack the nations or announce a conquest; instead, they took no notice of the humans, as if they did not even exist.

The Horde's machines landed all over the Earth to begin digging and extracting every ounce of metal from the planet. Giant constructs came from the heavens and latched onto the earth like the leeches that lived in the swamps that now covered any low-lying land. They sucked up raw ore, man-made tools, power generators, wire, and vehicles. They found anything that contained metal and took it.

The shamans of the day surmised that they were waging a galactic war and needed more raw materials. The Horde did not interact with the people in any way, treating them as pests that inhabited their latest claim. They processed the metals, precious and basic, out of all previously made products in their orbital smelters and dumped the nonmetal waste materials across the sky, raining down on the Earth for the next five hundred years.

The great chiefs of the day sent messages and demands, then pleas for the Horde to stop. No answers came. Men sent their powerful armies against the Horde, but they were ignored, except when their metal weapons were taken away, with no regard for the men using them.

The cities fell, forcing the tribes to become nomads and scavengers, living on the strips of arable land during the last ten years of the mining and for the subsequent half millennia.

Gunty was riding his juka beast through the canyons. The canyons crisscrossed the entire world, formed when the Horde had stripped away the land to mine deep into the Earth. Juka beasts had been winged passengers on the Horde machines; they had leaped off to scavenge. They resembled ancient reptile-like birds and could carry a small man.

Gunty was excited. At fifteen years old, he was one of the youngest to take to the air, and he had just pulled off his first raid. While the others focused on grabbing food and medicine, he had gone to the Harlum tribal chief's dwelling and found his prize.

The S'eak S'ell.

The S'eak S'ell was technology. It was powerful and known to help predict important events when used by a powerful shaman. The Horde had consumed most technology, but some items had survived. His own village shaman had ten artifacts from the past, and an eleventh would bring Gunty more standing in the tanasi.

Gunty had been smart during the raid; he had also found a sun-power plate with two wires. The wires themselves would bring the price of a small herd of livestock or two young juka beasts. The sun-power plate was priceless. When held toward the sky, it could bring technology to life, as long as the wires were good. Now the S'eak S'ell would work for his tribal shaman.

Gunty flew below the canyon rims so the others would not see him and try to take his prize. He returned to the cliffs; there, the flat land on top was reserved for crops and livestock, with the houses, workshops and other dwellings built into the canyon walls below. Gunty landed on a communal platform and ran to the shaman.

The shaman smiled as he took the prize, holding it aloft for all to see. He placed the panel, connected the wires, spoke an incantation. He touched the S'eak S'ell.

"Play," said the S'eak S'ell .

The people gasped. The shaman held up his hand for silence and touched the artifact.

"Now spell Water."

The shaman touched the S'eak S'ell numerous times and the S'eak S'ell said, "Correct; now spell blood."

The village cheered. They would have rain this year, but it would require a sacrifice.

Tom Tinney is a biker nerd and USAF vet with experience in radar systems, aerospace, and instrumentation industries. When not at work, he spends time motorcycling and writing for biker magazines, as well as conservative blogs. He now writes science fiction novels, his favorite genre to read (and watch). Ride safe. Ride often.

30. The Earth Is Dying

Jot Russell

"The Earth is dying," said Luke.

"What do you mean, dying?" asked the President.

"According to our best estimates, the desert's growth is accelerating by an additional fifty thousand acres a year. At that rate, it will span the planet and overcome even our most fertile land within a hundred years."

"How do we reverse it?"

Luke looked down. "We can't, sir."

The President jumped up, stormed around his desk and stared Luke in the eyes. "'Can't' is not in your job description. You were hired to solve this problem, and that's what you're going to do!"

The President walked past, poured a glass of water from the bar, and stared back at Luke from the wall mirror. He turned, bringing the glass with him. "You see this? This is all we need! All you have to do is extract it from the sea or from subterranean supplies."

"Our conservative estimates include our best efforts to desalinate water from the sea."

"Then we have to double our efforts," demanded the President.

"There's more, sir."

"This better be the good news."

"I'm afraid not, sir."

"You tell me the Earth is dying, and then you say that's not all the bad news you have to tell me?"

"I'm sorry, sir."

"Stop kissing ass and tell me what it is!"

"We're dying." Luke spoke with the words painfully escaping his lips.

"What the hell are you talking about?"

"The epidemic that's spanning the planet—it's not viral, it's something else."

The President let go of his anger and gave Luke a somber look. "If it's not a disease, what is it?"

"Its start coincided with the initial expansion of the deserts. At first, we didn't think the two could be related."

"You're saying the same thing that is killing the planet, is killing us?"

"It seems so, sir. The question to us was how? About twenty years ago, our navigational sensors stopped pointing north."

"I remember. What does that have to do with this?"

"We understand now why the compasses no longer work. Something in the Earth herself has stopped. Something that does more than direct our boats. Something called magnetism."

"I've heard about these magic rocks. Continue."

"We were able to reproduce the effect in an experiment. By spinning a large ball of iron, we were able to control the compasses. What's more, when we blew metallic dust at the ball, its course was partly diverted."

The President shook his head. "So, what does that mean?"

"We believe there is a massive metal ball in the center of the Earth. That, somehow, it was able to spin faster than the rest of the planet. And by doing so, it created a magnetic force-field around the planet that protected us from something. Something from space."

The President let out a deep breath. "Did you verify any of these results?"

"Yes, sir, in several ways."

"So what do we do? We can't just sit around and hope for some type of miracle."

"I don't think there is anything we can do, except to plant a seed."

"Plant a seed? You tell me we're dying, that our world is dying, and you want to plant a seed? What good would that do, when anything we plant here is just going to die anyway."

"Not here, sir. We've been experimenting with rockets. We think we might be able to send microbes or even small animal life to the third planet, Ocean. If we evolved from this life, perhaps we will again."

Jot Russell: An engineer is a designer of work to fill a purpose. Whether that be to build a tower that stretches into the sky, to create a soft parade of logic to command artificial life, or to find a way to arrange random words into the dramatic, those who seek design fulfill their own purpose. I'm an engineer.

31. Arrival

Karl J. Morgan

It turned out that the skeptics were right to question the motives of the alien fleet that appeared in orbit that late October day. I was sitting in my San Diego backyard, sipping a cold beer, when one of the ships blocked out the sun. Sirens sounded and the military went on alert, but what could a single man or all of us together do against their superior technology? I am one of the lucky ones, surviving in this cave far from the city and the invasion forces, watching the perpetual fires in relative safety. I am not a prepper, but I have friends who are and was lucky enough to join them when they bugged out.

At first, we were terrified the aliens would find us, but after two weeks, it seemed they had enough slave labor to carry out their mission to extract all natural resources for shipment to their home world. The media had gone silent, the Internet was permanently offline, and the cities not burned to the ground were dark, saving energy for the mines and factories.

I was certain Kyle had lost it when he said we needed to strike back. Somehow, he managed to form alliances with others groups and planned a series of assaults on the invaders. I knew it was a suicide mission, but could not allow them to destroy our planet while I cowered in the caves. It was no honor to inherit a dead planet. Better to die now and give those bastards something to remember.

Early on that fateful day, we began receiving encouraging reports from other groups. Casualties were high, but several alien installations had been overrun. It was just before dawn when we encountered the first alien patrols. The odds were heavily in our favor and the aliens were dispatched almost instantly. Now we had their weapons too. Kyle turned out to be a military genius and as lethal as a team of Navy Seals. By 10:00 a.m., we were at the gates of the alien compound, having left a trail of dead aliens and pools of green blood behind us. A thirty-minute mortar barrage and a hail of machine-gun fire later, we captured the compound. The surviving aliens were chained together and Kyle looked them over. I knew our victory would be short-lived, but these aliens would think twice before invading another planet.

"What is your name, Commandant?" Kyle asked.

"Balook Nizfaz," the tall, green alien spat, his black eyes blinking in the bright sunlight. "You know that reinforcements will come soon and you will all die, right?"

"Let me kill that bastard," I shouted.

"Calm down, Sid," Kyle laughed. "You're done killing for today." He glared at the alien commander and stated, "And there will be no reinforcements, Balook! Watch your friends abandon you." Kyle pointed skyward just as the massive alien starship shot upward and disappeared.

"What did you do?" the commandant demanded.

Kyle walked up to the alien and shoved him backward, knocking him to the ground. The other aliens formed a tight, protective circle around their fallen leader. At that, the ground around them cracked, and a massive flood of termites crawled out and surged over them They screamed in pain as their flesh and sinew was consumed by millions of ravenous insects. I could not believe my eyes, and moved back. Kyle was laughing out loud. Within a minute, only the skeletons of the aliens remained.

"What just happened here?" I gasped.

Kyle patted me on the shoulder. "Sid, there is only room on this planet for one invasive species. We've been here millions of years, which makes Earth as much our planet as yours. The last thing we will allow is some other planet coming to take what belongs to us, and that includes you, Sid." As I watched, Kyle's skin cracked and thousands of termites emerged and crawled down and back into the ground, leaving only the pseudo-skin of my former friend.

Karl J. Morgan is the author of the Dave Brewster series of science fiction novels and the Heartstone series of fantasy novels. The Hive was awarded an honorable mention at the 2013 Southern California Book Festival. He lives and writes in Southern California. http://www.karljmorgan.com

32. So, There

Allen Quintana

"Look at the sky."

They came in out of the southern galactic plane, a cloud of spacecraft, their beams slicing anything they lanced. Lines of white-hot fire cut through stone as easily as it did people.

Teardrop-shaped craft hummed in like waves of locusts, devastating all they came near. Buildings, trees, cars, avenues, and lives were turned into ash as the alien armada stormed the planet from horizon to horizon, leaving in its wake a fiery wasteland of slag and despair.

"We shouldn't have."

Forests raged aflame, as animals of all types fled in fear from the heat. Many more succumbed to the conflagration encompassing them, dying in the worst way, as did many campers caught in their midst. Bridges of stone charred and shattered, then collapsed. Arches of steel puddled, then melted and poured into lakes and rivers, the latter exploding into mushroom clouds of steam roiling into a once placid sky.

"Perhaps...."

Oceans boiled from the polar caps to the equator as heat beams raked latitudes. Sea life bobbed lifeless as columns of concentrated sun speared the waters into a cauldron from the depths to the wavetops. Vessels on the surface became pyres, before joining ruptured submarines below. Many islands fell to volcanism as heat rays skewered their once-extinct mounts. Continents were cut up like cakes; hundreds of miles of their coastlines sheared off and spilled into the waters before the seas burst into searing clouds.

"Talk to them?"

Homes exploded like soap bubbles, as if from a child's toy, as beams of fire furrowed cities, scorched towns, and torched neighborhoods. Larger buildings popped like balloons as needle-like bolts shredded streets and schools and shops. Mountains became mesas, then hillocks, and then craters as spacecraft weapons gouged the land in geometric destruction. Communications lines and wires were cut to ribbons. Surprise was complete.

"Maybe we should have."

People ran in panic. Many screamed as they never had, seeing strangers and friends and loved ones cut down by falling masonry or flashed away at the slightest touch of a white-hot shaft, right before their own ends. Above, teardrops hummed and rained destruction as teardrops of another kind slid from the dying below.

Nothing—and no one—was spared from the merciless invaders from the stars.

"Too late."

Then—there was silence.

What remained was a burning, smoking, pitted, lifeless world that once had thrived and flourished and harbored countless forms to be seen, heard, admired, held, loved. Now all was gone with the swath of an alien scythe from beyond that had cut the world to the bone and left a bleached skeleton of a planet dead in the cold of space, never to rise up and look at its stars again.

The humming from the teardrops stopped, as did the fiery lances, which had finished their toil. Thousands of spacecraft hung above the dead world for a moment, then all but one left, back the way they had come. All but one.

It descended to a spot, burned to glass, now cooled enough for landing. The teardrop alighted and all was silent there, save the burning breeze that carried the smell of smoke of the city, of flora, and flesh.

The teardrop sat there, then opened like a glistening flower, misleading to its destructive nature. Then two space-suited figures came out. Both aliens turned about and surveyed the work.

"You know, Mike," said one, "I really didn't want it to come to this."

"Yeah," said the other. "We didn't have any choice, Joe."

"I know," Joe said. He thought for a moment. "What was it that you called it?"

"Gimme a sec." The one called Mike wiped his visor of the wind-blown soot that dusted the landscape to the horizon. "Oh, yes."

He scanned a column of black smoke, its pall turning the sun a hellish red.

"An eye for an eye."

Allen Quintana is a California native. He doesn't need a "feminine side" since he's sided from all points of the compass by five daughters and his lovely wife of 24 years and counting, which inspires his muse with plenty of drama and humor and then some.

SECRETS

33. The Question

D C Mills

I attend the trial in disguise. Of course, I do just about everything in disguise these days, except maybe shower.

For today, I have chosen a vaguely military or Guard-style look: black bodyglove, high boots, crimson leather tunic. An embossed scabbard holding a short, pointed sword on my left hip, and a shoulder holster with two snub-nosed laspistols. Over it all, a long, black cloak with the hood drawn up to shadow my face. Probably an unnecessary precaution these days, but old habits die hard. The overall effect is intended to keep people from looking at me too hard, to avoid risking a violent response to their curiosity.

The trial results, predictably, in a guilty verdict, and the convicted girl is brought straight to the scaffold in the courtyard outside. The crowd pours through the wide doors, now flung open, to take advantage of the full entertainment package. Everybody loves a good burning.

I haven't seen who I came here to find, so I make my way upstairs to the private chambers of the higher officials. I go to the door with the right name on it, knock, and enter immediately, as if I really were an officer, taking access to any room for granted.

He is standing by the window behind his desk, reading from a data slab while making notes. I have, of course, been watching him for a while, but being in the same room elicits a response from long unused neural pathways. Old emotions awaken.

He looks up, surprised, annoyed at being disturbed, but quickly feigning politeness at the sight of my uniform.

'What can I do for you, officer?' He puts down the data slab to show cooperation. Sensible, even for a man of his rank. I wonder, briefly, if I can still trust him.

I pull down the hood of my cloak, releasing the holographic visor.

'It's me.' I say. 'I'm back.'

He stares at me, as if unsure whether I am real. I can't say I blame him.

'I have been mourning you for over a century,' he says at last. 'You were said to have died in the fire.'

The fire, indeed. The huge conflagration that destroyed not only our native city, but the surrounding countryside and neighbouring towns: most of the continent, actually, causing the ecosystem of the planet to tilt and slide over the edge.

'I'm sorry. It was safer to stay in hiding.'

'Safer? For whom?'

'For everybody. You, too.' I hesitate and then plunge in. It's what I'm here for, after all.

'I have been able to investigate, do undercover work. I believe I have found the cause for the destruction of Naxos, as well as the organisation behind it.'

'What do you mean, 'organisation'? It was the Enemy who destroyed our planet.'

'It would seem that way,' I say carefully. 'It was supposed to seem that way. The evidence was compiled and manufactured to point everyone at the Enemy—or rather, to confirm everybody's inherent suspicion that the Enemy was behind the attack.'

I hand him my data slab containing the details: times, dates, connections, code names. Plans and reasons, maps and lists. The insane rationality behind the planned destruction of a whole series of planets, an entire subsector of the galaxy.

'This is unbelievable,' he says. His eyes narrow. 'How can I be sure that you are you?'

I have been waiting for this question; I had expected it sooner. Is he growing old? Or feeling too secure in his position of power, maybe.

'Ask me anything,' I say. 'Or ...'

He looks at me shrewdly. 'A mind-meld? You know I wouldn't risk that without knowing it really was you.'

Long ago, when our world was still green, we knew each other intimately and believed it would be so forever. We shared everything. Some secrets are hidden so deep that even identity theft or torture cannot bring them out: only someone who already knows the answer can ask the right question.

I think I know what his will be.

I shrug, outwardly unconcerned. 'Ask, then.'

I brace myself for the coming wave of unleashed memories. Will my laboriously upheld balance of mind withstand the emotional assault?

He asks the question that will at the same time confirm my identity and be my undoing.

D C Mills (a.k.a. Dorthe Møller Christensen) is a scholar and teacher of classics; knitting designer, runner, reader, and writer of short stories. She lives in a small house in the middle of Denmark with three tall sons and a spoilt cat.
diotima.ktl@gmail.com

34. Alecre and Shanno

S.M. Kraftchak

Peering into the busy passageway, Creela practiced a respiration, tugged her uniform into place, and stepped forward. She walked slowly at first, her eyes darting to each humanoid that passed, smiling when they smiled, and returning nods.

"Lieutenant Creela, a word, if you don't mind?"

Creela paused. Looking around to be sure no one heard her hydra pulse quicken, she turned to face the tall man with blonde hair and blue eyes. She hoped she wasn't being rude enough to blush. "Major Hanson, what can I do for you?" He stopped close enough that she could sense his musky smell, and found it strangely alluring.

"I was going over your thesis on alien incursion and found your premise quite interesting. I wondered if you might be available after-shift to discuss it over drinks."

Creela spotted the corners of his smile quivering, as his pupils widened, and was relieved to know that humanoids couldn't hear her hydra race as she could hear his heart. She felt her mouth drop open as her mind scrambled to find the correct response. Think quick, Creela, think. What would a humanoid do?

"Um, um, do you think the environmental controls are malfunctioning? It feels awfully cool in here," she said.

Hanson's face creased above his eyes, and the corners of his mouth turned downward.

Creela hadn't yet mastered the complex language of humanoid faces. "I'm sorry. I didn't—"

"No, I'm sorry. I didn't mean to make you feel uncomfortable. Perhaps I should—"

"No, it's okay. I'm sorry. I've been alone in deep space for so long that my interpersonal skills …."

Creela smiled and held out her hand. "I'd love to discuss my thesis over drinks."

Her own eyes widened and she forgot to respire as Hanson lifted her hand to his lips and pressed their warm softness to her palm.

"Until later, then." His voice was a deep low purr.

As Hanson walked away, Creela tipped her head to the side to overcome a rush of vertigo. Her mouth formed a perfect O as she admired the man's sculpted form. "Well, let's hope our species have more than that in common," she thought. She was mildly aware when another humanoid stopped close behind her.

"You lucky girl," Yeoman Tate whispered in Creela's ear. "Every red-blooded female on the station has been yearning after that one. You don't even try and you lure him right in. If only he'd wear his uniforms a little tighter...."

"It's just a meeting to discuss—" Creela looked at Tate.

Tate snickered and fluttered her eyebrows. "You keep telling yourself that."

**

Looking both ways first, Creela pressed Hanson's door chime. The door opened almost immediately. Hot moist air surged from behind the man, who nearly filled the doorway.

"Lieutenant Creela, so glad you could make it."

Creela trembled involuntarily in the warm humidity.

"Come in, please."

She nodded and stepped in. The room was lit by a small, dancing holo-fire. She tipped her head as the man stepped in front of her and removed his flowing shirt to reveal his glistening chest. She never suspected that humanoid mating rituals were so close to her own. Creela felt her tiny spiracles nearly suck her loose clothing to her skin. She struggled for composure and held a hand to her cheek. "I'm sorry. I'm not feeling—"

"No deception necessary, Alecre."

Creela stepped back and stared into Hanson's face. "How do you know that name?"

Hanson eased forward, gazing into her eyes. "You are so focused on your deceptive form that you don't recognize me, do you? I'd know you across the galaxy by your essence."

Mesmerized, Creela allowed Hanson to lift her flowing shirt over her head. As it slipped from her arms, her spiracles flared. "Shanno?"

A moment later, their spiracle-covered skin flushed lavender and their bodies pressed together, allowing their essences to entwine in sensual embrace.

S. M. Kraftchak notes: As a writer who spends most of her time in other worlds with dragons, elves, and the occasional alien, S.M. still enjoys sunrise on the beach, sunset in the mountains, and portraying Elizabeth Tudor. She has two dogs, who think they are footrests, a cat who thinks she's a blanket, and three awesome daughters. Her husband is her best friend, her harshest critic, and her most fervent supporter. Writing is S.M.'s passion.

35. The Bold and Parenthetic—Dr. Emma Dash

Gene Hilgreen

The smells of wasteland, from long abandoned and burnt-out buildings—foul miasma of the Anacostia River—excited her soul. From the upper perch of her building, a swarm of mosquitoes circled Emma Dash as she stared at the dome of the White House—from the upper perch of her building. Each mosquito that entered her Kwan—an eighteen-inch invisible shield—dropped dead to the ground.

From the outside, it looked like every other disheveled building in the area. On the inside, it was a state-of-the-art Quantum Nanophysics Laboratory, and Em Dash, her preferred address to close friends and family—and long thought dead by the current administration, was exacting her revenge. Emma defended the Constitution—well, what once was the Constitution, but now was only a piece of art from the past with no meaning. The man who ruined her life went by many names (Barry, Obie, Barack, Soetoro, Soebarkah), and Emma knew them all. She knew his past and could prove it. The man she loathed more than anyone on Earth now went by—Harrison J. Bounel.

"How dare you challenge me—the Lord and Savior of America," he said.

"Yeah Barry—you may have the Fourth Estate, the far left, and Hollywood fooled, but—you don't fool me."

"Well, Dr. Dash—you're fired." He turned to walk away, stopped and nodded to his Secret Service detail. "In fact—arrest her. Dr. Emma Dash—you are done!"

Three months later, with mounting support from the right, her bail was set at twenty-five million dollars. An anonymous admirer paid it and she was free.

Em Dash faked her own death—

She watched as the full moon shone blue-white over the White House dome. But enough with her sightseeing—she had work to do. That same moon shone over her neighborhood, thronged with gangs at war, the drunk and dissipated, adventurous students of debauchery, as well as the lonely, desperate and deformed—all there for her picking. Her robots extracted them from the grim and foul-smelling lodgings that they called home.

Dr. Emma Dash had perfected her own drone, a programmable biomechanical mosquito that would attack its designated target, and she was fully prepared to target American citizens with drones. One of the many flat screen monitors arrayed on her desk displayed the late edition of the Washington Post headline—Extra, Extra Twenty-Second Amendment Abolished—President Bounel Declares Marshal Law.

She looked to her army of human-like robots and said, "Get me three more subjects."

There were many reasons she choose this site for her lab. The proximity to the White House was important, but the plethora of homeless subjects, and access to the river—for disposal—were the most important. She was never concerned with her own welfare; her army of androids protected her from any person who dared to encroach on the programmed boundary, which defined her sphere.

She turned her attention to the story in the news that followed the headline. From the White House lawn at 0900 hours on August 13—tomorrow morning—in celebration of International Lefties Day, President Harrison J. Bounel would declare to the world his new self-appointed title—Supreme Lord and Ruler of the United States of America.

Em Dash smiled and yelled out loud, "Never going to happen!"

At nine a.m. on August 13, three unwitting spectators awaiting the president's speech unknowingly released a swarm of deadly mosquito drones. Within seconds, Harrison J. Bounel was dead.

Dr. Emma Dash—her boldness apparent—smiled.

Gene Hilgreen spent thirty-five years in information technology and ITGC audit. Now retired, he authored Dragon at 1600, the first of a series in which he lives through his protagonist Buckner Axele Davidssen, a protector of the Constitution ... who reports only to God and Old Glory.

36. Arctic Freeze

Kalifer Deil

Mason Dodd, a salmon fisherman out of Scanlon Bay, had the Bering Sea as his mistress. It challenged him with its tree-tall waves and screaming winds, making him feel alive. He caressed it when it was glass-calm and the Chinook salmon seemed to jump onto his hooks. When he was on shore he felt uneasy, in a foreign land with people he didn't like. His boat, The Big Chinook, was his home, his refuge, his country.

He set out Tuesday morning on The Big Chinook, a custom Blasedale Sportfisher, constructed of heavy carbon fiber, unsinkable, self-righting, and providing the comforts of home. He set a course to his favorite spot, 70 miles east of Nunivak Island, and went below to sleep off a hangover. He never drank at sea but always in port to shut out the people. The only person he tolerated was Mike, a buyer who knew salmon.

When he awakened Wednesday to a sea of blue-green glass and air minus 6 Celsius, a thin sliver of sun could be seen that spread on the horizon. He walked out on the icy deck, holding onto the rail with his gloved hands. Realizing he would be at the area soon with 12 lines to set he went back to the cabin, filled his pockets with trolling sinkers, wrapped his right arm around a set of poles, and grabbed a can of live bait with the other. He set all the poles into their sockets, circled back to bait the hooks, and attached a sinker.

While he was baiting the third pole, the boat heaved and the bait can took off toward the opposite gunnel. He dove after the bait, so the trip would not be a loss. The ice on the deck made no attempt to slow either Mason or pail, so both hit the gunnel together. The round can, now on its side, became a wheel, flipping Mason over the side under the railing. No life jacket, a pocket full of sinkers, going down, and before losing consciousness he was enveloped in a blue-green glow, "Bioluminescence?" he thought.

Mason awoke in a room with an indiscernible light source. Puzzled, he yelled out, "Am I dead?"

A familiar voice answered, "No." It was Mike, now walking toward him.

Mason, still confused: "Mike, where the hell am I?"

"Your mind's been resurrected. We were inspecting an ancient crash site; then we surfaced under your craft, causing you to drown. Your body is dead."

Mason looked down. "I have a body."

"A virtual body, and all else can be what you think it to be."

Suddenly Mason found himself on his boat. "I did that?"

Mike was standing on the deck in front of him. "Yes, I'm your memory of Mike, with alien help."

"You mean space alien? You saved me?"

Mike faded, saying, "We fix what we cause."

He wished for things as they were, and he was on the deck baiting hooks. The boat slowed to troll, dropping all lines. Mason was beginning to think all that happened was a dream.

A little impatient, he thought, "What if they all bit at once?" Then, all the lines flexed. He jumped from pole to pole reeling in the salmon, 12 beautiful specimens, and 40 pounds each. He repeated this twice and returned to Scanlon Bay.

Mike was there, since Mason radioed him. Mike yelled as he docked, "So, you had a bit of luck today." Mike, amazed at the catch: "These are perfect."

It all felt real. He thought himself younger; he was. He thought huge Chinook salmon; he pulled in a 120-pounder. He thought the best-looking whore in Anchorage, Trixie Card; he had sex with her. He thought Joe Grundy, a fisherman he hated, fall overboard and die; he heard the commotion by radio: when pulled from the water, Joe was dead. Mason smiled.

He couldn't die. He could wish anything.

Mason thought, What if I think something impossible like this boat flipping over and not righting? He noticed a rogue wave on his starboard side but failed to notice another on the port side. The starboard wave crashed into the boat, flipping it; then the port wave hit, an instant later, crushing the boat between them. The remains quickly sank. In the darkness of his dimming mind, he heard Mike's voice, "We can rescue you from our mistakes but not from your own folly."

Kalifer Deil is the writer pseudonym for Gary Feierbach, a Silicon Valley engineer. He writes mostly hard science fiction but occasionally branches off into occult, fantasy. He also writes science articles and has a website, http://www.kaliferdeil.com, with curiously interesting science articles and some short stories.

37. The Duplicate Goodbye

Jon Ricson

Ergo sat on a large pipe near the airlock. Through the portal window, he saw the Jure, his beautiful second home. He'd be aboard her for quite some time, so it was a good thing he thought of the ship so fondly.

Looking back into the busy port, he saw his To-Be-Beloved approach. Not until she neared did he notice that she had done him yet another injustice.

They had been Predestined for several seasons, but it had not been easy. They were not well-paired. She was from one of the most traditional families on Padar, who did not appreciate his more progressive proclivities. His decision to undergo a transform was especially troubling for them, even though Solian transforms had become very popular across the entire planet.

Onni was also disgruntled that her To-Be-Beloved was about to take off on yet another monitoring mission near the Sol system. Traditionalists had been quite vocal against the Padarean obsession with the Sol system since the first transmissions had reached Padar many seasons ago.

"Ergo, you look … well." The voice was cold, but that was not uncommon for even the most advanced of the robotic Duplicates. The fact that she had sent her Dupe was yet another slap in his face, a face she had more than once seemed to regret looked more Solian than Padarean. The "nose" and "ears" were the hardest for most Padareans to look past, as Padareans had only slits in those areas. The eyes, too, were different, rounder and more colorful than those of Padareans, and had he seen her actually shudder the last time they were together?

"Were you precluded from coming in person, my Predestined?" Ergo looked into the cold screen that held the visage of Onni's face. Her narrow gray eyes showed no reaction to this.

"I was not feeling well, and did not wish you to take any ill effects to share with your shipmates."

He pursed his lips, something a Padarean couldn't do since they had none. "We will be away from each other for some time; I would think this a reason to be here in person."

"May we speak in Pad, please?" Onni said, tilting her head in frustration. Solian English had become quite popular, first as a cultural phenomena, spoken only by the more affectionate of the first Solian broadcasts that had reached Padar, including and especially the one about Solians trekking through the stars. But, over time, it had become a popular if not dominant language, spoken all over the planet. Traditionalists detested English too, of course.

"Is this better?" Ergo responded in the dominant Padarean tongue, clicks and all.

"Yes." Onni looked away, distracted from the viewer, but the Dupe did not turn. She was looking off-screen, something considered rude in Dupe relations. She quickly faced forward again.

"Well, I hope your journey is successful. I apologize again for not being there in my full form."

"You are forgiven, my Predestined." Ergo grabbed her hand, or at least her hand by proxy. He tried his best to look at her with hope, but knew this was probably not their last goodbye.

Onni managed a thin smile. "Goodbye, Ergo. Safe travels." At that her Duplicate withdrew its hand, turned, and walked away.

He turned, as well, and looked out again at the Jure. At least "she" would welcome him. And perhaps there was something out there waiting for him that would make this separation from Onni all worthwhile

Jon Ricson writes science fiction, detective, and other entertainment literature. He resides outside Orlando, Florida, and

you can often find him walking the streets of Disney or Universal soaking in the creativity.

38. Hank and Rosa

Nōnen Títi

Exhausted, soaked through, and short of breath from the climb against the ice-cold wind, Hank and Rosa finally reached the top of the rocks above the beach. There, way below them, on the edge of the water, lay the means to their survival.

"She looks so small," Rosa shouted over the noise of the wind in her ears.

"Hurry," Hank answered, taking her hand and pulling her downward over the sand and rocks that littered the treacherous Queen Maud Land coastal flat, across which, from all directions, people and animals were heading towards the only refuge that would stay afloat while the super storms raged over the planet and drowned the earth.

One after the other, the storms had terrorized the land for almost ten decades now. Large portions of the continents had sunk. A hundred million people had drowned in the last year alone. Entire populations were on the move, searching for higher ground—where they were not welcome.

At times, Rosa had longed to see the places Mum and Dad so fondly remembered from before—places like San Francisco, New York, The Netherlands, and Bangladesh—but they were long gone.

The scientists had issued warnings, which the United World Government, from the safety of its Himalayan offices, refused to take seriously. One of Mum and Dad's colleagues at the South Pole Science Observatory, Sibyl, a self-proclaimed prophet, had started to build their refuge on the new coast, a coast that had not existed until recently and yet was perfectly drawn on the map Rosa now kept safely hidden under her clothing—the ancient map of sea admiral and cartographer, Piri Mehmed.

At first, Mum and Dad had dismissed the idea of the looming disaster, until multiple cyclones and hurricanes started to form simultaneously, each fuelled by the increasingly large oceans that resulted when most of the polar ice melted, and each coinciding with the full moon. They had still trusted the technology when Sibyl had announced to the world that these storms would collide in a super storm that could wipe out humanity, and that she was willing to save only as many people and animals as could fit on her refuge.

Only when the solar storm plunged the entire planet into darkness, devoid of any working equipment, had Dad taken the map from the observatory museum and handed it to Hank and Rosa. "Run and don't look back. They're not going to wait. Use the map as payment; find the raft and save your lives," he had said.

Hank and Rosa had not had a chance to think about it, no time to say goodbye. Nobody knew how much of the land would sink from under their feet; the key was to get to the refuge. There had been no time even to be sad and think of Mum and Dad being left behind for the sea to swallow.

Rosa felt her eyes go hot at the memory. Civilization seemed so far away and so long ago, yet it was only three days since they'd left the observatory; three days of walking, using the map to guide them, with only water and biscuits to sustain them, until the refuge was now only a few hundred meters away.

"Have you still got it?" Hank asked her again.

Rosa nodded, holding tightly on to him with one hand and clutching their precious map against her chest with the other. "What if she won't accept us; what if they want to avoid inbreeding later?"

"She won't know. The solar storm blew out all the equipment; there's no data."

Rosa nodded and concentrated on not falling over the rocks, while watching the last animals enter the ship. She was so tired, but there was no time to waste, so they started running again until, finally, they reached Sibyl, who welcomed them as she kissed the map and hurried them aboard.

From now on, they'd be at the mercy of water and wind; no Gulf Stream left for direction; no weather prediction without satellites. Yet they would float, while the continents sank, one by one.

Nōnen Títi (www.nonentiti.com), pen name of Mirjam Maclean, is a writer with a background in health care, education, and philosophy who writes fiction and nonfiction books inspired by the inborn differences that influence the beliefs, behaviour, and natural talents of every person.

WENDING

39. Did Curiosity Kill the Cat?

Andy Lake

Well, the headline writers couldn't resist it, could they? 'Did Curiosity Kill the Cat?'

As head of the Mars Exploration Research Centre, only I know the answer to the mystery that has puzzled the world since that strange discovery. And by the time you read this, it's a secret I will have taken with me to the grave.

I still remember the excitement that day 15 years ago, when the Mars Rover Curiosity found bones on the Red Planet. Extraterrestrial life had been found!

And then—the discovery of further remains that were, quite clearly, a cat. The media said Curiosity had run over the cat. The first roadkill in outer space.

So who put the cat there?

Theories multiplied. The Chinese had been conducting secret missions, sending animals to Mars. Aliens had abducted life forms from Earth, then somehow mislaid one on the way home. Perhaps time-travelling humans had visited Mars, or Bastet, the Egyptian cat-god.

One crank cult believed a species of future felines, the creatures we evolve into over the next 10,000 years, traveled through time and lost one of their infants there.

Of course none of this is true. The truth is more prosaic, yet also bizarre. It goes back to 2003, when I was senior engineer on the Beagle 2 project—the most expensive flop in the history of the British space programme.

We had such high hopes. Beagle 2 would be launched from the orbiting Mars Express. It would bounce to a safe landing on Mars. It would open up its clam-like structure, and send back a rich vein of data about the Red Planet. But we lost contact with it after it separated from Mars Express—and that was that.

What went wrong? Investigations suggested a problem during descent. It fell too fast, and burned up. Its parachutes failed to open, or airbags failed to deploy. Its design was insufficient to withstand the heat, velocity, or impact. All logical, but incorrect.

In reality, the problem started in Baikonur in Kazakhstan, on launch day. As usual, we were in a flap. I was late. On the way to the Cosmodrome I saw on the side of the road a sack that seemed to be alive. I stopped the taxi, and went to look. Inside the sack were three young cats, in a pitiable condition. Being an animal lover, I took the cats with me. On arrival I gave them some milk in the kitchen, and left them in the care of a cleaner.

You've guessed the rest. Somehow, in our busy-ness, we let down our guard. Somehow, in our final check, one of the cats crept in and, I suspect, got into Beagle 2's protective shell.

My joy at the successful launch turned to unease when I only found two cats in the rest area. Discreetly I hunted high and low, but one had gone.

Truly, as they say, no act of kindness goes unpunished. Doubly so, in this case. The poor creature I tried to rescue must have been dead soon after take-off. And the Beagle failed, at huge cost.

Maybe its weight put all our calculations out of kilter. Maybe its oozing body juices seeped into the electrics. Who knows exactly?

But how I winced whenever someone used the word 'catastrophe'. I blushed with shame when economists talked of a 'dead cat bounce' during the recession.

I kept it all to myself, hoping the cat had slipped safely away before take-off. But when Rover sniffed out the cat's bones ten years later, my fears were confirmed. Still I kept quiet.

I am not proud of this. Every day, when I look in the mirror, I see a man who is not a great and revered scientist, but a fraud. And yet .... If I had owned up, my career would have ended, at no benefit to mankind. I made the mess. I should clear it up and take us forward.

And standing behind me in the mirror, I see the shadow of bungling, hubristic humanity.

So I know we will go on, making a hash of everything we touch, undermining our hopes by our stupidity, then covering up our crimes and follies in the hope of profit, or in the self-deceiving hope of making amends. Onwards to the stars, my friends!

Andy Lake's day job is researching, writing, and advising companies and governments about the future of work. When he takes his suit off, he writes about the future of anything. His futures are full of many opportunities which we subvert through our ignorance, recklessness, and idiosyncrasies. In short, "the future is something other than what is intended."
http://www.andylake.co.uk

40. Back To Basics

Joanna Lamprey

The brief, three years ago, had been electrifying. Interstellar travel was a reality, with the first exploration ship due to launch in five years. Nick Taylor had been one of three thousand experts pulled onto the project, and the years since had been the most exciting, exhausting, alarming, and thrilling years of his young life.

His section covered crew wellbeing—even at interstellar speed, the closest promising-looking planet was four years away. The ship would transport a team of experts, spend a year on the planet—all going well, of course—and return. Most of the passengers would travel in stasis, since it wasn't logistically possible to provision up to ten years for so many people, but the minimum crew of nine—three at a time on duty, 24/7—was their main worry. How could nine people be kept from going stark staring mad in eight years, during the hours they were neither working nor sleeping?

The section personnel were gathered today for an update on that vital issue, rehashing the many suggestions that had been tabled—revolving all the personnel in and out of stasis, or choosing only crew who shared a single language; loading ship databanks with thousands of films and books; hurriedly inventing a Voyager-style holodeck. That one never drew many laughs; it was so obviously what was needed. Entertaining a crew, even a multilingual one, wasn't the impossibility; relaxing them, however—the five volunteer teams living in trial conditions were all stressed almost to incoherence within months.

Overall coordinator Tom Burkett tapped a pen against his glass for attention, and the heated conversations died. "You'll remember at the original brief we invited some SF writers, in the hope they could think outside the box on this? We've got a presentation from William Robertson coming up next. We'll go through now."

William Robertson! Nick had been a fan all his teens, still was if he had time to read, and craned eagerly over the heads of the people walking in front of him for his first close-up glimpse of the author.

Robertson was taller, heavier, and older than anyone in the room; he nodded unsmiling greetings as they entered the room, where nineteen chairs were grouped around a steel fire bowl. Fire? Nick took his place with the others, and Robertson, leaning on one of his trademark sticks, bent to touch a lighter to the bowl.

Flames leapt and Burkett spoke up. "No talking. Relax and watch."

This was stupid—there couldn't be an open fire on a spaceship!—but Nick watched obediently. His frayed nerves eased; he could smell wood burning, and an elusive faint trace of something else. Someone, presumably Robertson, threw a chunk of rock salt on the fire, which sparked and burned blue. There was something else … people, shadows against shadows, and the plaintive strains of a harmonica. Horses snorted nearby, and stars burned huge in the night sky. One of the men threw a log on the fire in a flurry of sparks—

Nick flinched, and was back in his seat.

"How the hell did you do that?" he exclaimed involuntarily. The others were looking equally startled, and Robertson grinned into his tidy beard.

"Since we first learned to summon fire," he rumbled, unexpectedly Scots, "it has been our comfort, our safety, our dreamy pleasure, triggering our most primal feelings of wellbeing. I released a permitted narcotic—milder than a wee dram—to prime you. The crew will have the same narcotic. Imagination—memory—you'll have all experienced summat different. And will, every time you look into the flames, no matter how often you look. Our trial team use it a few times a week, and their stress levels have dropped back well below concern levels."

He swung his stick at the fire pot, which flickered as the stick went straight through the image.

"It's not real?" Ann Moore wasn't the only one to gasp, but she was the only one to speak.

"Och, it's real, burning right now, and it will for the next two years. Every flicker, every added log, all captured on holographic film for the journey. Smoke and mirrors, ken? Smoke and mirrors."

Joanna Lamprey lives in Scotland, near Edinburgh, mainly writes whodunits set in the very beautiful area surrounding the Firth of Forth, under the name E J Lamprey, and will one day achieve an alien amateur detective who solves murders brilliantly. One day.
http://www.elegsabiff.com/sf-microstories/

41. Escape

Andrew Gurcak

Heat, stench, water, violence—everywhere, all the time, no escaping for Boseda. His earliest memories were of being chased by Area Boys across the plank bridges that joined the houses and shops perched on stilts above the open sewer lagoon. Maybe he was a Beninese orphan, abandoned along a street or waterway. Someone must have shouted a name and he answered, or he didn't and they beat him until he did. So he was Boseda of Makoko, of the worst slum in Lagos.

Boseda survived through quickness and wiles—enough, barely. When he began to pluck melodies from the din around the shacks and stalls, and not only mimic but expand them, his life got better. And then better. At first, he hummed and sang to himself just to have one thing, one nice thing, in his control. His sometime friends started pressing him to entertain them. He hit on the idea of stopping in front of a stall, starting a popular song, then improvising extravagant riffs. Passersby paused to listen and the shopkeeper would hustle them for a sale, tossing the boy a few coins. Boseda soon began demanding coins upfront, began scheduling his stops, and finally was trawled by an A&R exec from a local recording outfit. They first had him cover foreign hits, but soon he was fashioning his own songs with wildfire success—Nigeria, next sub-Saharan Africa, then worldwide. He needed only one name, and Boseda became one of the wealthiest entertainers on the planet.

He was vastly amused by his successes, and whenever reporters interviewed him, he would first chat at length with them, gauging their story slants, then spin out what would most entertain them, laughingly waving off inconsistencies. What people called truth was to him no more than a choice at a crossroads—always his to make and dependent only on where to go next. That, and from childhood, the odds of being caught, if he chose poorly.

Boseda enjoyed his wealth, but more his ability now to explore the wide world. It was the late 21st century, after all, and he was determined to learn from others as excellent in their fields as he was in his. He befriended technologists and became obsessed with breaking out of what he sometimes saw as a life grown no less cramped than that of his boyhood. He began talking to anyone who would listen about actually sailing to a star. "The road to any star can't be harder than mine from Makoko to London." He grilled experts in interstellar propulsion and suspended animation, discussing with total earnestness such an adventure, however impossible the odds of success. He would travel solo, and would not be dissuaded by wise people warning him of his dreams' foolishness.

He liquidated his fortune to bring together the minds most capable of building him his starship. He invented misinformation and ploys to maintain secrecy, but his fame fast punctured those schemes.

Plans were assembled, prototypes built, failures accumulated, and lessons learned. At last, he had bankrolled the best vessel he could, and outfitted it with the most capable AI, navigational, survival, and musical gear possible.

Boseda was determined to have no coverage of his launch. Equally determined news organizations, however, obtained crude amateur footage from technicians showing Boseda entering the hatch, then the craft lifting off. Telemetry reads showed all systems activating as designed for the solar slingshot. From Boseda, uncharacteristic silence. Over the months, he transmitted only snippets of observations and wonderment. As he neared the sun, data reported an irremediable malfunction in the ship's AI. The navigation failed to recover, and with the last words the earth would hear before his sunfall, Boseda assured his listeners that he had chosen the right road, no matter. He would die ablaze and smiling.

About that same time, a man so ordinary one could scarce remember his face came into a small town somewhere in Africa. He hustled gigs singing in bars. He had a pleasing voice and patrons would urge him to try for the big time. He demurred and lived a long, happy life there. He was appreciated for two traits: riffing effortlessly on any phrase, and needing no audience to applaud his act. He rather seemed to prefer an empty room to a packed house.

Andrew Gurcak and his wife, Elaine Lees, divide their retirement time between Pittsburgh and the Finger Lakes region of New York. The Science Fiction Microstory Contest entries are his first fictional pieces. agurcak@yahoo.com

42. New Chinatown

JD Mitchell

——Y̲ou sure look uptight, mister. You going to a funeral or something?—

Wernher wished things could work out that simply. They couldn't. Not today, not ever.

—Not really, sir. Please watch where you're driving. —

The cab careened over the newly-laid causeway's rubber surface. Wernher wanted to say the ride reminded him of the autobahns back home. But the cabbie was a Chinese refugee, and you just didn't see people like that in the Socialist West. Not with the Big Berlin Wall.

—Hey, don't worry about me, mister. I learned to drive from a G.I!—

Wernher looked out the window as the last of the Marina merged into the Mudflat District. New Bay Street's columns flew by at a fast clip. A blur of speed.

—Can't you go faster, sir?—

Already, the traffic hemmed them into the lanes on the causeway. There was barely any room to make it around other flivvers.

—You're crazy, mister. Everyone on the coast is coming for the USS Hornet. Even the president will be here!—

Wernher knew that wasn't true. MacArthur would stay far away from this event. His advisors wouldn't have wanted the scandal to tarnish his reputation.

The causeway looped around the projects of the Mudflat district. The grand land-filling of the Bay continued. Lamps from the night shift workers bathed the sides of the temporary brown tenements. The flivver's "fifth" electric wheel made sparks against the causeway's wires.

—Why you in such a hurry, anyways, mister? The astronaut's speeches will last for hours.—

Wernher half-listened. He took his mind off the scenery of filled-in Bay Area sprawl, the webwork of canals, and trains of container ships. In his hand, he held a tooth—the tooth of Jacqueline Bouvier—the only proof he had to implicate astronaut Michael Collins.

The cabbie looked back at Wernher in the rearview mirror. They made brief eye contact. Most likely the cabbie was a refugee of the very brief Sino-American War.

—It's a pretty big deal, huh, mister?—

For a second Wernher feared the cabbie realized the significance of the tooth. The cabbie smiled. Most of his teeth were gone. Radiation sickness....

—It's a big deal, right?! What the astronauts found, right? Proof of life on Mars.—

Wernher felt relief cover the terror on his face.

—Oh ... oh yes.—

Sure, Wernher thought. It made everything worth it. The Apollo Applications Program. And the murder of Jackie.

New Bay Street's terminus was ahead, at the end of the causeway's slope. He could see the Golden Gate Bridge. BART station New Embarcadero. An aircraft carrier was docked at the wharf.

—How much do I have to pay you to get me right ... there ... at the foot of the stage?—

—Right at the stage?—

He pulled out a stack of hundred-dollar bills and held twenty of them out like a fan.

—You got it, mister!—

Wernher smiled.

The cabbie engaged the gasoline tank and drove off the causeway, onto the street, and into the BART parking lot. A crowd of thousands upon thousands cheered enthusiastically for the returning heroes of Apollo 13.

Wernher jumped out.

The noise of the applause was deafening. Michael Collins, the first man to step foot on Mars, spoke at the podium. Applause washed out his voice. Wernher dashed up the steps. Then he felt a sharp weight of pain in his back. Then another. He saw blood.

The crowd cheered.

He stumbled, fell back, looked down the steps. There was the cabbie with a smoking gun. Wernher could read his lips.

—Forget it, mister, this is Chinatown.—

JD Mitchell has been a writer since he first played with Legos. Since then, adventures as a butcher and teacher have inspired and informed many of his narratives. His main interest lies in the origins of science fiction, specifically as a way for him to study the problems of the present day. jeffreydavidmitchell@gmail.com.

43. Under the Slaveways

Jon Ricson

I reach up and push in the stuffers. They barely keep out the waves of sound from the roads above. The above world of the Primes. Their shiny world with automated roads, abundant food, freedom, safety ...

Down here all we get is the noisy turbines, cast-off sparks from the slaveways above, and the darkness, even in the daytime.

The world above calls us Strags, when they call us anything at all.

I made a job for myself. I find stuff that Primes cast off, then sell it to black marketeers. They pay good for slaveway or hover parts, foodstuffs that fall down here, or other Prime things like commlinks or jewelry.

Looking up, I watch the hovercars whiz by, never ceasing.

I feel the vibrations of the huge steel supports that hold up their world. I feel it in my teeth.

Then I push my cart towards the next open area.

They used to call this area The Loop. My momma once said this used to be one of the bigger cities in the world. Now Chicago Prime is the city. We live below in the old world. We are just the Strags. Life is hard down here.

I see some dark figures ahead. I know who they are.

They yell at me, so I pull one stuffer out. I can barely hear them screaming.

"Hey you," one of them says. "What you got today?"

"Not much yet," I say. A large transport rushes by overhead.

They push me around a little. They see I just got started. They move on. I push the stuffer back in my ear. It's just a dull roar now.

Regular Strag folk come out of hiding as the gang leaves. So many. They look at me, wondering what I got, but they don't cause trouble. They are just hungry too.

I walk towards a ray of light coming through the slaveways above. I feel the sun on my face. I wonder what it's like up there in the sun all day. I wonder what it's like to be a Prime.

My momma once told me she and some friends went up there in the old days. That was before Strags were told to stay down here. That was before The Laws.

Momma said that once Strags lived with Primes. She said in the old days Strags weren't even called Strags, they were just folks with no homes. But eventually there just was too many of us.

The Primes wanted a world without us. They wanted a new shiny world.

Something reflects the sunlight near my feet. I pick it up. It's a little girl's bracelet. Momma taught me to read a little. It says "Marcey." I like that name. If I still had a sister, I'd like that to be her name. But she died. Strags that get sick don't get well that much. Just like Momma said.

I look around to make sure no one sees I have the bracelet. Strags don't have much that's shiny. That's for Primes.

I know it would probably bring good trade from the black marketers. Maybe even real food from Chicago Prime. Maybe some meat—hopefully cow and not dog. But I like the shiny bracelet that says "Marcey." I want to keep it for awhile.

One of the stuffers comes loose and the whooshing traffic above fills my ear. I push it back in.

Time for me to move on, before the gang comes back and finds what I got. Time to see what else I can find today under the slaveways.

Jon Ricson writes science fiction, detective, and other entertainment literature. He resides outside Orlando, Florida, and you can often find him walking the streets of Disney or Universal soaking in the creativity.

44. Martian Hoard

Lars Carlson

"**I**t will suit our purpose?"

Olaf Ivarsson, Viking jarl and thane of the late king Bjorn Jormunson, stood on the prow of his longship while regarding two men standing on the white sands just ahead of its beached prow. One hand rested on the hilt of his sword while the other stroked his great braided brown beard.

"It will, jarl," gasped one man, crouched on one knee and breathing hard behind a gray cloth face wrap. "Not a sign of any man about and as forbidding as the African desert. We could not hope for better."

The second man, standing tall and leaning on a gnarled walking staff, nodded assent. Unlike Olaf and his retinue, this man wore heavy robes of blue and gray.

Ruddy dust covered both men.

"Very well," Olaf said. "Beach the ship and unload."

The rest of Olaf's retinue clambered from their rowing benches. Half jumped the gunwales into cold black water gleaming with reflected starlight to muscle the warship fully onto the shining beach. Those remaining aboard lowered the mast so that it would not snag on the many stalactites jutting from the starry darkness. Both groups passed cargo from the vessel's center once the ship was made fast.

Olaf labored beside his men to see the task done.

The robed man circulated among the jarl's company while they worked. He handed to each man gray cloths like that the dust-covered scout wore; intricate golden wires and matte blue nodules laced their hems. Veterans of Olaf's black-water expeditions thanked the robed man and set the cloths about their faces. Vikings new to the matter were instructed in their use by the robed man's keen, sibilant voice in hushed tones.

Within an hour, Olaf's company set out from their landing. Pairs of them carried heavy chests and crates, marching up the shining sands toward a dim orange tunnel hollowed from the starry night. Passing through it the Vikings found themselves on a scree-covered mountain slope beset with red dust. The sun shone small and cold in a yellow sky.

Olaf's men muttered uneasily amongst themselves.

The Viking jarl ordered them quiet; they obeyed.

In wheezing silence, the company marched, following their scout and the robed man. The way was not difficult, but whether from the dust or the mountain's height (dust obscured its lower slopes), they all labored for breath. The Viking's shirts of iron rings and the burdens they carried did not help them any. Stops for rest were frequent.

Eventually the company arrived at a pile of boulders. Pleased with the site, Olaf directed his men to dig. A trench was excavated in the dry, red dust and the cargo laid inside. This cargo represented the best of Olaf's latest raid on the Irish coast as well as the bulk of his wealth. With King Jormunson dead, some of his jarls sought to make themselves king in his stead—or just take tribute like one. Olaf had no intention of seeing his riches stolen. He hid his treasure to recover in better times.

Olaf's company erected a small cairn at the foot of the boulder pile to mark the site. In this, Olaf laid a broad silver baptismal bowl, looted from a Britannic church years ago. He'd marked the rim with his dagger.

When this was done, the Vikings rested briefly before marching back to the black-water beach. They were eager to set sail for home, to see the blue seas again and familiar fjords.

***

What did one say about such a find? What could one say? No one in the Curiosity Mission Control room knew.

The big monitor showed the rover's main camera staring at its own dusty, distorted image in a neat pile of rocks. Days prior, the rover spotted a twinkle on the Gale Crater's outer slope and came to investigate. Scientists expected some kind of crystal formation, hoped for ice. They found a silver bowl bearing Scandinavian rune-marks and a cross defaced into a Thor's hammer emblem.

The next day, a translation of the bowl's runes was received from a Norwegian college: HERE LIES THE HOARD OF OLAF IVARSSON, TO BE CLAIMED BY HIM OR HIS KIN.

Lars Carlson is a welder, network administration student, gamer, and avid reader who sometimes manages to find time to write, every now and again (just not as often as he would like). He currently lives just north of Seattle, Washington, after 27 years as a native Minnesotan.

45. The Ghosts of Gale

Allen Quintana

" and—and, then he said, 'I'd sure like to try that in zero-gee!'"

The confined walls of Hermes One shook against the laughter as the pair punched the bulkheads with the soft edges of their fists or butted them with the backs of their heads as they threw back laughs at the tasteless joke.

"Jeez, Joe, that gets me every time!" said Benson, wiping a tear away. "That never gets old."

His partner yukked; his grin was ear to ear.

"Even after forty years."

The guffaws trickled down to chuckles, then light laughter, then titters, eventually pooling into snickers, and finally evaporating into silence.

"Well," said Joe.

"Well," said Benson.

"What's happening outside?"

"Same old red," Benson said. "Wanna look?"

"Nah," his partner voiced. "Call me if you see a rescue ship," he said unenthusiastically.

"Will do, commander," said Benson. He craned his neck at the window, and then twisted again with a grunt, at an awkward angle, to peer at the back of Hermes One via the mirror, which gave him that rear-view. "I sure could swear I saw something out there."

"Uh, huh," the commander of Hermes One nodded unconvincingly at his crew of one. Joe then smiled to himself and looked back 200 million miles and wished he could go back and change his mind. He and Benson had been the prime crew for the flight, deemed secret and experimental. The NERVA rocket was only a prototype

146

and worked too well for orbital trials. What was supposed to be a wide Earth orbit and a splashdown after a few days got extended when both Houston and the crew couldn't shut down the engine. Hermes One went well past its intended flight path. He and Benson never could get an answer from Mission Control about why the flight computer was programmed for a Mars window. NERVA (Nuclear Engine for Rocket Vehicle Application) worked too well, all right.

"There it is again," said Benson, contorting himself to get a better angle from the mirror. "Just beyond that ridgeline."

"Sure," said Joe.

"Really, Joe, take a look."

Joe hated two things about looking outside. First, the bad angle was more trouble than it was worth. Their ship lay on its side with a list that offered a bad view of the landscape, and it hurt to cant oneself for a look. Second, Mars never changed; the view was the same. No trees, no fall colors, just permafrost now and then in rust-colored desolation.

There was a piece of the sky, Joe could see. A line of clouds scudded westward like a wagon train from another time and another place. The pastel hues reminded him of Janet, who would have adored the pinkish shades, the dominant color of her bridesmaids' gowns, which she so loved and he so hated. Off in the distance, a row of rusty mountains had been weathered down for uncounted eons by the thinnest wisps of air, air that carried dust to coat everything to the outside of every nook and cranny and crevice of Mars, and to the inside of every crumple and crack of crashed Hermes One. No, there was nothing new out there. The same as it always was. How he longed for home and for Janet, for he hoped they were still—There.

It slowly came over the ridge; a cautious track of its wheels slowly purchased each inch of ground that gave underneath. Time meant nothing to it as it slowly panned the landscape with something new to see.

"Hmm," observed Joe. "Curiouser and curiouser."

With every inch, every turn, every pebble of Gale Crater over which the wheels spun, the thing came closer to the ship. The discovery of the crash site didn't strike the thing as shocking or give it even a passing fancy. It lumbered at the same slow pace as before.

"There's nothing alive in there," said Joe.

"Doesn't matter," said Benson. "There's nothing alive in here, either."

The robot poked its electronic eye into the shattered window, past the cracked, weather-worn mirror off to the side of the long-gone-cold wreck.

It was here that the lonely Martian winds for time uncounted had whipped a-frenzy its red dust in its high, opaque altitudes, skittered across its salmon plains, and wafted over its crimson, barren peaks. For here is where its fine grains had finally settled, more recently on the remains of the broken shell of Hermes One, burying what they could.

And also on those within it.

Allen Quintana is a California native. He doesn't need a "feminine side" since he's sided from all points of the compass by five daughters and his lovely wife of 24 years and counting, which inspires his muse with plenty of drama and humor and then some.

46. Unnatural Harmonics

Karl J. Morgan

The day they arrived was neither the disaster authors had imagined nor the scientific boon academia had suggested. Massive starships hung like cumulonimbus high in the atmosphere, casting surreal shadows over the Earth. The ships were not metal military masterpieces, but instead were soft, gelatinous blobs that seemed incapable of traversing space. Millions panicked, while most prepared for the inevitable Armageddon when the aliens landed.

Yet the ships just hung in the sky for days, turning into weeks without activity. "What are they waiting for?" became the most common phrase spoken. After the third week, people tried to get back to their lives, since they had to work in order to eat. After five weeks, life resumed its natural course, even while governments tried to find solutions to the situation.

It was early on a Tuesday in the eighth week when something changed. Small moss-green vessels left each starship and landed in the center of every large city. It was noon in San Diego when odd figures emerged from the ships. They looked human, but very tall and thin with green skin and moss-like hair. The aliens walked away from their ships and stood waiting while crowds formed around them. The same scene played out everywhere. Where it was night, lights were set up. Where it was raining, free umbrellas were handed out.

At 2:00 p.m. San Diego time, the aliens spoke in the native language of each city. "First, we need to apologize to you," the aliens said. "What has happened here is our fault and we freely accept and acknowledge our responsibility. It was probably inevitable that you would enlist unnatural harmonics in your desire to learn and grow. But now we have discovered it, and are here to fix the damage."

"I don't understand," shouted a voice from the crowd. The alien walked over to the young man standing just behind the barricade. "What have we done wrong, and who are you to tell us to change?" the man asked.

The alien laughed out loud. The glint in his eyes and the teeth in his mouth seemed completely human. He reached out his green arm and touched the man on his shoulder. "What is your name?"

"My name is Dave Brewster."

"Hello Dave. My name is Pando Krakus, and I suppose I am your brother. We colonized this planet long ago. On my planet, people evolved to look like me. On this planet, humans evolved to look like you. There are many human species in the galaxy. The one thing we have in common is our refusal to allow unnatural harmonics."

"What does that mean?" Dave asked.

Pando frowned. "Look around you!" he shouted, waving his arm at the skyscrapers and at the concrete they stood upon. "You have corrupted Nature's sacred balance. These structures were built with unnatural harmonics and must be eliminated. It is an atrocity to subject this globe to such acts."

"But these are our homes and places of work," cried a woman from across the circle. "Where shall we live? How can we survive?"

Pando walked back to the center of the circle as a deep guttural rumble began. "The natural harmonic you hear will continue for several rotations, continually gaining volume. After the third rotation, decibel level will be powerful enough to disassemble the unnatural harmonics. I suggest you use that time to distance yourself from these things. We cannot protect you if you stay here. Once the natural balance is returned, we will come back with new technologies to help you."

An old woman standing next to Dave Brewster screamed and fell to her knees. He knelt next to her as she clamped her hands over her ears. Then he yanked her hands free and pulled out her screeching hearing aids, which dissolved into dust in his hands. "You can't do this to us!" he begged the alien.

"Leave the city now. Your atrocity is at an end," Pando snarled, pushing his way through the crowd and boarded his vessel, which lifted off noiselessly and headed back into the sky.

Karl J. Morgan is the author of the Dave Brewster series of science fiction novels and the Heartstone series of fantasy novels. The Hive was awarded an honorable mention at the 2013 Southern California Book Festival. He lives and writes in Southern California. http://www.karljmorgan.com

47. Fox, Cat, Fireworks

Jeremy Lichtman

"Roman Candle drives are simple things," declared Wilbur. He brandished a large adjustable wrench in his right hand. "The mathematics are hairy, I'll grant you that, but the machinery itself is trivially simple."

He made a small declaratory tap of the wrench on the base of the auxiliary capacitor bank. "Tesla could have built this," he added, further clarifying his intentions with a slightly harder tap.

"Sir, you're likely to get your jacket covered in grease," said Fox, attempting to divert Wilbur's attention , and potentially avert tragedy. "If you'll allow me, why don't I take a look at it while you chart our course?"

"An excellent idea," said Wilbur, heartily, and handed the wrench to his valet. "Wouldn't do for us to run into a big rock, or some such." He headed forwards to the ship's relatively luxuriously appointed bridge (it had leather command chairs).

Fox adjusted his monocle, then thought again and placed it in his outer jacket pocket. "Here kitty, kitty," he said quietly so that Wilbur wouldn't hear him. The man doted on the cat. "Damn cat. I bet it urinated on a wire or something."

He fished in one of his trouser pockets and drew forth a small treat, which he waved around in what he thought might be an enticing manner. A pair of furry ears protruded from behind some bulky, chrome-plated machinery.

"Tsk, tsk, here kitty, kitty." The entire cat cautiously shimmied forth, keeping a safe distance from Fox. Neither trusted the other, with cause.

Fox waved the treat around a bit more, then tossed it through the hatch and into the corridor. The cat stared at him for several long seconds.

Fox jerked, as if he was about to launch himself at the cat. It twitched slightly, but didn't move, calling his bluff. "Enough of this," he said, and charged at it.

"Not that direction," he muttered, catching himself on a large brass pipe to change his momentum into a different direction. The two of them circled the room several times, the cat obviously moving with far greater alacrity.

Triangulating, he managed to cut it off so that the exit hatch became its safest escape route. It hissed at him. "What?" he said. "Get out of here. Scat! Go have your treat." It left, with a dirty look backwards at him. Fox shut the hatch behind it.

He reached into his pocket for his monocle. Not there. He patted several other pockets. Not there, either. Must have fallen out. He peered around nearsightedly. After several more moments of futility, he fished out a small, collapsible pair of glasses, unfolded them, and perched them on his nose instead.

"Where were we?" he asked himself. He went over to a corner and picked up the wrench. He must have thrown it at the cat during the chase, although he didn't quite recall doing that.

"Aha," he said, spotting the problem.

A few minutes later, he popped his head into the bridge. Wilbur was engaged in a testy conversation with the ship's AI, which insisted that it knew the correct route.

"Sir?" asked Fox, attracting his attention. "I found the problem. There were mouse droppings in the engine room. Must have come aboard with those passengers you picked up on the last trip. Filthy buggers. They ate right through some wiring. The mice, I mean, not the passengers."

"No wonder Pelly has been back there so often. I know you don't like him very much, but you have to admit he knows his job."

At that point, a bell rang, telling them that their ship's plasma cloud had charged sufficiently. The AI acted first, before Wilbur could send them off course, and they leaped forwards into the abyss in a cloud of furious sparks and electrical   discharges.

Jeremy Lichtman is a software developer, based in Toronto, Canada. He writes in his spare time, in moments intended not to incur the wrath of his family. http://www.jeremylichtman.com

48. Ordmak

Kalifer Deil

At night I could hear her song echoing in the mountains. It was like a thousand singing voices calling me. It was beautiful, mystical, and it aroused an inner yearning that was new to me. My mother said I was coming of age and that I would be experiencing new feelings unfelt before. Maybe this is what she was talking about.

It was a new day and I needed to gather ice-radish at glacier edge. It was a long trek, but one I had made many times. There were rumors that there was much ice-radish on the slopes of Cave Mountain, but that was the home of Ordmak. It was closer than glacier, but I was told her song was irresistible and Ordmak would eat me for breakfast. A children's story. I was sure. "It was just the wind playing the caves like organ pipes," I self-spoke.

As I reached the upper slope of Cave Mountain I saw many caves, which told me I was right and ice-radish was plentiful as well. As I approached one of the larger caves, I heard the voice of Birgo whisper to me, "Hi, Greimo!" He disappeared three weeks ago and was assumed eaten by Ordmak. I entered the cave and, as my eyes adapted to the dark, I noticed bones piled along the side of the cave. Then a dim flickering lit up the cave wall from behind me. I turned to face a creature longer than I could see, with one large eye and a gaping mouth with luminescent walls. It was propelling itself with wavelike motions of its frilled underbelly. It stopped a ways away and my fear turned to amusement. It had no appendages to grab me and the mouth was devoid of teeth. I also knew I could easily outrun it.

I heard a chorus of voices from its mouth, some familiar, of friends who went missing, and others I didn't recognize. I said, "Are you Ordmak?" It answered, "We are all Ordmak." I was then engulfed in a mist and was instructed to take my clothes off and throw them into what appeared to be a fire pit. My body complied even though my mind said no. Then I went into the mouth as instructed and it closed. Every cell of my body became like my male protuberance and I was engulfed with extreme pleasure. It was beyond anything I could have imagined.

I found I could see out of Ordmak's eye as he spit out my bones. That thought soon evaporated as I found myself in the company of many others. Birgo took my hand: "You are in the universe of Ordmak's mind. You just fed him so you will have ten lifetimes of pleasure. There are babes here I'd like you to meet."

I just realized that I missed my mother and would never see her again. "Birgo, I really miss my mother. She warned me about Ordmak, but I thought it was a children's story."

"Don't worry, she will be here soon. You will call her," Birgo explained. "Now check these out. This is Makin and here is Makin's mother, Milda."

"They look the same age."

Bilgo responded, "In here everyone is the same age. You and I are both older and more mature."

I looked down and noticed my protuberance was larger; then I looked over at Milda and felt my protuberance become firm.

Bilgo started to laugh. "We are all nude, so there is no hiding place for your feelings."

Milda took me by the hand and said, "Let's join a circle-of-eight."

It turns out the circle is more like a sphere of eight of us joined in a copulative manner. The sphere pulsates in and out more and more rapidly until a climax, when it blows apart and we all go flying. It was sensuous and fun and we repeated it several times.

Later I heard my mother calling, "Griemo! Griemo!" and I instinctively answered, "I'm in here!"

Very soon I saw her approaching me; she was nude and her body was in her late teens. I grabbed her hand and said, "Mom, let me introduce you to a circle-of-eight." She didn't resist.

Kalifer Deil is the writer pseudonym for Gary Feierbach, a Silicon Valley engineer. He writes mostly hard science fiction but occasionally branches off into occult, fantasy. He also writes science articles and has a website, http://www.kaliferdeil.com, with curiously interesting science articles and some short stories.

49. Conservation

Andy McKell

We turned the corner of the ancient riverbed and saw more of the same insane greenness—oh, how I had come to hate that color. This piece of jungle was another chaotic mess of green upon green. Again. It was just more of the same—part of this same hell. And we were finished. We could go no further.

Here, where the trees had not yet managed to enclose the sky and the full glare of the midday sun lanced through to add to our misery ... here, our search, our holy quest, was silently abandoned.

The guide, ever enthusiastic, dropped his pack, jabbering as he ran forward pointing at something, some things, that eluded us. Things here, there, and over there.

We stared hard into the blazing green-hazed glare; a couple of the women even tweaked at the corners of their veils. We saw nothing but the endless overgrown, buzzing, biting, poisonous jungle that we'd battled through and hated for weeks. What had this solid team of seasoned conservationists become but a loose and bickering assembly of personal and collective defeat?

No, we still saw nothing but more of the same.

It was enough—done, finished, over, failed. But the guide kept jabbering and pointing ... some of the less-defeated reluctantly drew towards him. Others gazed around, lost. The rest collapsed to the foetid floor in despair.

Then our disbelief melted a little. Perhaps there was, after all, something ... some things ... there? Our cautious, unbelieving shuffling slowly turned to a more enthusiastic pace, staggering against and over the boulders and fallen logs, careless of hidden beasts and toxic orchids.

Suddenly, we became a ragged line of madcap, headlong, rushing lunatics as our pattern-seeking inheritance reasserted itself. Was that a ninety-degree angle? Could that stump indicate a crumbled tower? Was that a suspiciously straight line emerging from within the tangled growth? A building? No—buildings. Many buildings.

We began pointing, yelling out "Here," "There," "Over there!" Crazy people. The guide grinned a knowing grin, perhaps silently thanking his own gods for his lucky break: crazy people.

It was a city. Gorgeous moss-covered, frond-encrusted angles too sharp even for this insanely cruel jungle to have randomly thrown up. A city–our city.

We rejoiced. We stood in silent awe. We fell to our knees and offered up thanks. We lost our senses.

And then the long work of conservation began.

It was as expected. Long, long ago, all the fabrics had rotted; the useful metals had oxidized or leached away, even the perpetual plastics lay buried under meters of mulch.

But that mattered not—we had found the fabled ruins. The holy city from the elder days. We could clear away the jungle and all its dangers, scrape away the moss, spray preservation chemicals over the remaining stonework, build a railway from the coast, set up hotels, and stalls at a respectful distance ... our joy was immeasurable.

We were truly, finally there at the legendary lost city so holy that they named it twice—New York, New York.

Andy McKell is a new writer of speculative fiction, whose short stories are starting to appear in various anthologies. He retired early from the IT world and enjoys acting when he gets the chance. Married with three daughters, all pursuing careers in the visual arts, he currently lives in Luxembourg, Europe. andy@andymckell.com http://www.andymckell.com

PERCEPTIONS

50. Yood Must Find Itch

W.A. Fix

Above the equator and over what would someday be called the Pacific Ocean, a vessel containing two beings began to enter Earth's atmosphere. "Yood, my love, we are traveling far too fast. The vessel will break up in the lower atmosphere."

Yood began retracting the fibers, which made up his body, from those of his mate, Itch. "If we are separated, we will find each other again, and on that day our rejoining will be as the first." Yood and Itch continued retracting thousands of fibers until only one fiber remained of the union. In that one fiber all emotion, all thought, and all sensation was shared. Then, as predicted, the vessel broke into two pieces and severed the final thread of the joining.

Yood's half struck the planet in a swamp forest north of where New Orleans would eventually be located. Itch was carried another eight hundred miles north and east. Both were damaged and both took several years to learn that nourishment was obtained by simply extending volumes of fibers into the open air and absorbing the required elements. They eventually learned to hang the fibers from the local vegetation in clumps, and then extend new fibers to another location. In that manner the two began the search for each other. Unfortunately, the planet already had a mute life form so similar to their fibers that it confused even Yood and Itch with first contact. They would cautiously extend a fiber, hoping to find the other and offer the greeting, "Wobee (Wife), have I found you?" or "Dee (Husband), have I found you?" And so the search continued for nine hundred years. Then

Yood sensed a structure. There was some kind of wonderful vibration that emitted from it every day at mid sun. Wanting, ... no ... needing to be closer he extended himself and reached for a very slick surface built into the structure's side. That surface seemed to amplify the vibrations from within. Just before mid sun, Yood touched the slick surface and waited.

***

Inside the cottage a man sat at a grand piano. He shuffled through a stack of sheet music and extracted today's selection, "Rhapsody in Blue." He opened the music, placed it in the stand, then opened the keyboard. His right foot found the pedals and his hands hovered above the keys. He began to play.

***

The vibration struck Yood in every fiber of his being. The sensation was so intense that nothing else mattered and the need to get closer became desire. When the vibration stopped, he slowly came back to consciousness. Then faintly, from another part of his being, he felt a touch and he sensed the greeting, "Dee, have I found you?"

"You have, my Wobee," said Yood.

"It has been so long, my love, let us begin the rejoining," she said.

"Wobee Itch, let us just hang a while longer. I have found something new."

"But Dee Yood, you promised me the rejoining," she said. "What will become of our Wois?"

There was a gentle movement in his fiber, as if a light breeze had blown through. "I. ... We have a Wois? Where is she? What is her name?"

"She has gone to the south in search of her own way. She and I are connected as you and I are now. She feels your touch as strongly as I do. She is named Smee."

"I have a Wois," said Yood with great pride. "Wois Smee." He was flooded with a new set of emotions and the consciousness that was Smee. However, before Yood could recover, the wonderful vibrations began again inside the cabin, and this time Yood, Itch, and Smee were swept together into the rapture.

If it were possible at that moment to see all the moss on all the trees in the southeastern United States, about half would have been moving in time to music coming from a small cottage just south of Atlanta.

W. A. Fix (a.k.a. Bill Fix) is a retired information technology manager, who lives with his wife and three cats in the suburbs of San Diego, California. He has "toyed" with writing all his life and recently became more serious about the craft. Other interests include photography and golf.

51. The Recruiters

Joanna Lamprey

"I'm afraid it's out of the question." The Daolan looked apologetically around the four men facing him.

Admiral Hansen leaned forward. "Because we're from Earth?"

The yellow-skinned alien hesitated, then inclined his head. Humans have met many strange variations among the intelligent space-travelling races, but Daolans, acknowledged as the finest navigators of all, are odder than most, with a gelatinous body shape that can change at will. The Daolan had braced himself into a sitting position with four pudgy tentacles, and used two more to make gestures. The upper part of his sac-like body was fringed with silky follicles, which moved of their own accord as though sniffing the air.

Admiral Hansen looked round at the others, then back. "Gorman, we brought you here at some expense for this interview, you must have known we would be asking you to join our crew. I'll be frank—we were really excited that you agreed to meet us at all, so this is a great disappointment. I accept you won't take the job. I would like you to explain why, because yours is not the only race keeping their distance. "

Gorman shrugged, his follicles rippling, but answered honestly. "Earth people have already accrued a reputation for a certain, uh, oddity. I wanted to meet you, because I didn't believe it could be as disturbing as I'd heard, but ... you say things that don't make sense, then look at each other and pull faces. Sometimes you even make odd noises. It is—unsettling. Each voyage lasts at least twenty epochs; I think in your calendar that translates to a year.

To be unsettled for that long would be deeply distressing, so I have to say no."

"He means joking and laughing!" Smith realized." I once tried to tell a Gannan a pub joke, changing it to a Gannan, a Doonong and a human entered a bar—he looked at me as though I was deficient."

"What, you guys don't laugh? So a pompous, very dignified Daolan slips on a banana peel—okay, okay, forget banana peel, slips—and is suddenly on his back with his legs waving in the air—you don't laugh?" Jackman smirked and looked round for support.

The Daolan looked disgusted, all his nostrils pinching. "I'm afraid you just made my point."

Hansen shook his head at Jackman, annoyed. "So, your children—do they play? How do you know when they are enjoying themselves?"

"They jiggle, and their follicles vibrate. Sometimes their tentacle ends change colour."

"And does that disgust you?" Hansen persisted.

"Of course not."

"But it would be unsettling to anyone who wasn't a Daolan."

"Yes—which is why our young put aside such things when they are of an age to meet other races, at least in public. It is something entirely private."

"Well, our smiling and laughing is the equivalent of your jiggling and vibrating. Does that help?"

The Daolan pondered, then nodded. The admiral scrawled quickly on a piece of paper and handed it over. "Would you at least look at our offer?"

The Daolan took it delicately in a tentacle and read in silence. Then to their astonishment he started to shudder, and the follicles on his upper body started to vibrate. The tentacle holding the paper turned blue, then purple, and the admiral grinned fiercely.

"Oops," he remarked, "I gave you the wrong paper. Here's the real offer. I think you're going to fit in just fine."

Joanna Lamprey lives in Scotland, near Edinburgh, mainly writes whodunits set in the very beautiful area surrounding the Firth of Forth, under the name E J Lamprey, and will one day achieve an

alien amateur detective who solves murders brilliantly. One day.
http://www.elegsabiff.com/sf-microstories/

52. Reprisal Lucre

Lars Carlson

Light puffed against the stars.

"Lost contact with the Rio, sir," the tactical officer reported.

Vice Admiral Voan swore. Rio was the third destroyer lost, half of her screening force, and the cruiser Hamburg was making best speed away from the engagement zone on a power plant teetering on failure. That left her with five effective vessels to continue the engagement with the jyajub—including her own badly damaged heavy cruiser Nanking.

The vice admiral ran the numbers in her head. Between standard deployment fees, combat pay and the Commissariat's Heroic Image bonus—she glanced to her right to see that the ship's commissar was still on his feet and handling his camera—her force would break even, after the engagement.

Assuming they won, of course, without further losses.

Allowing the camera a heavy sigh, the admiral silently thanked the Lords of the Void for Avenger Bounties. At the rates the survivors of the Versas Massacre posted, she could still come out ahead.

"All done, sir," a medic beside her reported.

The vice admiral nodded and dismissed the man. Bandages encased most of her right arm now, soaked with blood beneath the tattered remnants of her greatcoat's sleeve where shrapnel caught her. The commissar's camera captured that side of her from beneath the admiral's command pulpit, giving her greatcoat's gold buttons and the smoke-stained lance-in-tsunami badge of the Blue Union Navy on her breast a grim human contrast to their dull shine in the bridge emergency lights.

Victory demanded bold action.

"Captain!" said the admiral.

"Sir!"

The captain of the Nanking stood from his command seat below the admiral's pulpit. He bled from a brow cut, yet that seemed only to enhance his command presence.

"Are there ASOs ready?"

"We have three available tubes, all charged and loaded," the captain replied.

"Prepare to fire, captain," Admiral Voan said, playing up for the recording. "Let's not let them get away with Versas or the lives of our brave comrades."

"Aye, sir!"

The Nanking's CO sat down and issued orders via his console.

Klaxons shrieked throughout the ship. The Nanking's computer warned the crew of the impending launch. It repeated twice.

Vice Admiral Voan fixed a suitably steely glare towards the main screen.

A jyajub Killship (nine klicks of scrap conglomerated in a web of cables, screen projectors and weapons) wallowed in space as the remnants of the admiral's flotilla flitted about it like angry hummingbirds attacking a boar. The Killship streamed debris and atmosphere from dozens of places but continued to fight.

That ship had participated in the deaths of a billion and a half inhabitants of Versas (against a slightly higher pre-Massacre number) and cost Vice Admiral Voan two months of hunting and four ships. It had to die before it did any more harm.

"Firing."

The Nanking "klunked." Recoil rams thundered. Lights flickered across the ship. An ozone stink filled the air.

"ASOs away," the tactical officer reported. "Terminal in two ... one ..."

Built for taking out asteroids and space stations and similar slow, predictable objects at distances greater than one AU, the ASOs were poor choices to attack maneuvering starships.

Usually.

Accelerating towards the distracted Killship and light speed, two of three ninety-ton chunks of ferrous-clad tungsten found their mark. They blew through the Killship's screens and hull, erupting out the far side in cones of silver flame. Seconds later their nuclear seed charges detonated, devouring the Killship's husk in clumps of golden sunburst. It was a thorough and beautifully photogenic kill.

Cheers erupted across the Nanking's bridge.

Vice Admiral Voan smiled. She didn't think much of vengeance as an ideal, as a goal, as a way of life, but she could appreciate its loosening the accounts of those desiring it. The dead of Versas had been avenged—as had the admiral's expenses.

Lars Carlson is a welder, network administration student, gamer, and avid reader who sometimes manages to find time to write, every now and again (just not as often as he would like). He currently lives just north of Seattle, Washington, after 27 years as a native Minnesotan.

53. Beta Test

Tom Tinney

The Lord saw how great the wickedness of the human race had become on the earth, and that every inclination of the thoughts of the human heart was only evil all the time.

The Lord regretted that he had made human beings on the earth, and his heart was deeply troubled.

So the Lord said, "I will wipe from the face of the earth the human race I have created—and with them the animals, the birds and the creatures that move along the ground—for I regret that I have made them."

But Noah found favor in the eyes of the Lord.

—Genesis 6:8

***

"Hey, Jidard, how's it going?" Pelban said, pulling up a stool at the Space Terminal passengers' recreation bar.

"Not bad, not bad. Just finished the prototype run on the CB-2675 Cloudbreaker system with my partner, Kirdol," Jidard replied, pointing his second tentacle toward the third member at their end of the bar. "Ran like a champ."

"Really? So you're ready to present it to the council and get a production license?" Pelban signalled the bartender for another round. Jidard flicked his gill slits, indicating yes. "You kept that under wraps. Where did you do your beta testing?"

"Well, that is a story," Jidard said, chortling through the air-holes that ran down his back. "You know that we have to test in the "life-zone," but the league says you can't screw with environmental factors on planets in League Territory or uninhabited worlds where life already exists? Well, ... we went outside the League."

"Wait. You went out into the spiral arm and tested? That must have cost a lot of credits."

"It did. And it was boring. No intelligent life for 50,000 light spans. Took ten friggin' spans to find a test planet, but we did. Took 140 spans to spool up and then we balanced the T-wave. We had 120 percent efficiency, so we are golden."

"That's great," Pelban said, regretting not investing in Jidard's startup when he had the chance. "I guess it's time for some fun now, eh?"

"Oh ... we had fun," Jidard said, pointing to his partner Kirdol and waving him over closer. "He is a creative type and has a killer sense of humor." They both broke out in laughter, drawing looks from the rest of the bar.

"Really. OK, let me in on the joke. What's so funny?"

Jidard indicated they should huddle closer. "I am not admitting to breaking the Indigenous Interaction Restrictions, okay? Nothing leaves this bar."

Pelban bobbed his feather crest, but his multifaceted eyes narrowed. "Do I want to hear this?"

"Oh, yes, you do. We were bored out of our minds, during the spool up, so Kirdol drops a spy-bot down the well near a village of the less hairy primates that seem to be over-running the planet. He runs a translation on the indigenous language. We are listening and we realize they are pretty simple and really gullible." Jidard and Kirdol looked at each other and laughed again.

"Ok. Enough. Get on with it. What did you do?" Pelban asked, his curiosity piqued.

"Well, when we are 120 spans from the end of spool-up, Kirdol ... what a pisser ... he sends a bot down with a holo-projector and voice comp. He tells this Indie ... what was his name again?"

"Noah," Kirdol said, speaking for the first time.

"No-ahhh," Pelban sounded out, and then shook his head.

"Yeah, Noah. Kirdol tells him that the world is going to end in 60 spans. He tells him to build a giant boat and get two of each animal on it because we are going to destroy the world in a flood."

"You ... what?" Pelban exclaimed. "Did he do it?"

"Yep. Finished just in time for us to turn on Cloudbreaker and rain on him for 40 planetary spins. The area we encircled with a repulsor field filled up and he floated around until we pulled the plug, 40 rotations later. Man, that boat must have stunk." They both laughed again.

"So, we got to prove that Cloudbreaker works like a champ and we drop mucus every time we tell the story again. It's a win-win."

"You two crack me up. The next round is on me."

Tom Tinney is a biker nerd and USAF vet with experience in radar systems, aerospace, and instrumentation industries. When not at work, he spends time motorcycling and writing for biker magazines, as well as conservative blogs. He now writes science fiction novels, his favorite genre to read (and watch). Ride safe. Ride often.

54. The 2000 Parade

Richard Bunning

"**B**ugger it, I feel right old today. Why the heck do I always agree to lead the march-past, Molly? Just because I was born on the 1st Jan 2000 doesn't make me special. What with that and the Water Wars Parade in September, anyone would think I liked bleeding walking. I watched the Remembrance Day march on Sunday. Parades all look the same, except we don't get the King at ours, just a few old political farts. Can you remember what Tommy Titmarsh asked me, love?"

"No, should I? It is a long time since I really listened to you, Dad—since I was about twelve, Tommy's age, actually. He'll learn!"

"Well, anyways, he said, 'Why don't you lot have your march on the 1st Jan, rather than in November, so close to Poppy Day? Give folks a break from that stuff on the News.' "

"So I tells him, 'It is right cold and always bleeding raining, even in November, without we old buggers freezing to death in January. The first few years we did do it in January, but we were all only 50 years old then.' "

"He says, 'Well it ain't like we get snow no more', cheeky bugger. Well, none of us are going to perambulate around in January at our age. Anyways, who the hell hasn't got a hangover on New Year's Day? It's amazing, a 100 and some years on, who'd a thought a century ago that there would be so many from the last millennium still about?"

"And a right grumpy lot you are and all."

"Ah, you just wait, my girl. Just 89, why you're still in your prime! I may be a fossil, but I'm still driving. Proper cars and all, not these modern things that run on fresh air and bleeding water. I've always been a petrol-head. My pride and joy is my DB5, well, you know my replica, and even it's nigh on seventy year old in its own right. As I've always said, it's the very car they used in the remake of Die On Yet Another Deadly Day. The proper roar of its engine, it's bloody magic. I'll never forget last year, what a malarkey."

"You are lucky to still be here, Dad."

"Put the kettle on, love, whilst I chat to myself, as usual."

"Put it on yourself, you lazy old codger."

"Pass me my stick then, there on your right, leaning against the table."

"There you go."

"Can I get you a bite of that cannabis cake while I'm up?"

"You shouldn't eat that stuff when you're planning on driving. You know what the cops think about spaced-out drivers."

"Just eases up the old joints, love. My knee gives me jip when getting down in the old girl's bucket seat."

"Well, you should get yourself a proper vehicle, Dad."

"Anyway, where was I?"

"About to tell me, yet again, about being James Bond."

"That's right. You remember when that young ****** hijacked me? He thought it a right laugh sticking that shooter in my face. Any road, there I am heading into London to get as near to the Cenotaph as my centenarians pass allows, that be Waterloo. Well, more like right back at the Imperial War Museum! Any road, at least it is easy for the Underground to Embankment.

Did you know that they built the Northern Line way back in the 19th Century? Anyway, where was I? As you know, this egit got into my car, keeping the gun on me all the while, and tells me to teach him how to drive, so he can nick it. Bloody cheek, how am I meant to tell him just like that how a bleeding clutch works, let alone all the other stuff? Haha ... huup ... I can't stop laughing. If the young twat had seen any of them old 007 films he'd of known about the ejector seat."

"Yes, and Dad, you were right lucky to get away with self-defence. You'd better not be doing that again."

"Don't worry. I can't afford to get the seat loaded right. It is nigh on impossible to find people with the right engineering skills nowadays."

"Never mind, drink your tea. I will come as well and make sure you get on the Tube safely; then I'll do a bit of shopping. That's if you promise me the ejector really won't still work!"

Richard Bunning is an author of speculative fiction. He has also published reworked neoclassical plays, a totally daft gift book, and short stories in a mix of genres. His best-known book to date is Another Space in Time. His website, geared towards the support of independent authors across many genres, is http://richardbunningbooksandreviews.weebly.com. richard.lw.bunning@gmail.com

55. What's Past Is Past

Sam Bellotto Jr.

BaxterSlug44 cast its largest eyespot in the direction of DocSlug123, blinking in amazement, and gurgled, "They had penises way back then?"

"The male forms did," explained DocSlug123. "A hardened tubular fleshy extension with which the male forms passed genetic material into the female forms. That was how they reproduced. That's what they called them."

The dig was located 130 jaglumphs past the Melted Region and 20 jags to the right of the Double Ditch, inside one of the caverns that pockmarked the whitened landscape. A few normantodes skittered about, but other than those smelly pests the area was devoid of life. This particular cavern, the structure, the unique way the winds whistled past the cracked rocks, provided a nearly hermetically sealed environment against the eons.

"Must have hurt like a sonofablarg."

DocSlug123 sloughed. "Repro is painful. Has always been. Nonetheless, we've seen evidence the ancients may have enjoyed the process."

"Yer shelling me?"

Another one slithered out of the cavern, smaller but a lot fatter, glistening with mucus. "Youse gotta see this!"

"LarissaSlug5. Calm down. You're drooling on my tail," DocSlug123 scolded. "What do we gotta see?"

LarissaSlug5 shifted its eyespots in the direction of the cavern. The other two followed it inside, past smooth and perpendicular walls, into an inner room strewn with an assortment of mysterious apparatus in remarkably good condition. On a circular bearing surface stood a two-by-three maug rectangle. The rectangle had an opening at the base in which discs could be inserted.

"We know this because we've tried it," said LarissaSlug5. It took a disc in its extensor and shoved it into the rectangle's opening.

Momentarily, the rectangle lit up and displayed moving images of two ancients. They did not seem to be wearing clothes. The ancients were writhing and slipping around each other like twistersnakes on a cold evening. "That one there"—LarissaSlug5 pointed out the ancient with a long, hard, fleshy tube popping from its midsection—"we believe is the male. The other is the female. It has no tube appendage."

"Yes," agreed DocSlug123. "The female one, however, has two fleshy mounds under its head. The male one doesn't have those."

"Well, glom your eyespots on this," LarissaSlug5 chortled.

The ancients continued writhing, a dance of skin and hair and sweat. Then the male ancient could be seen stuffing the flesh mounds of the female ancient into its own mouth hole. The female ancient did not protest.

"Is the male one eating the female?" asked BaxterSlug44 incredulously.

"We're not sure," LarissaSlug5 said. "It is possible. Feasting during a mating ritual is not unknown. That could be the purpose of the mounds. If so, they grow back rapidly."

"Not unlike our own dorsal puffs," noted DocSlug123.

Dorsal puffs were survival adaptations, sources of food and water in extreme emergencies, usually self-ingested, but there were stories of sharing sustenance.

"Interesting," BaxterSlug44 commented.

"Wait," advised LarissaSlug5.

The male ancient, having had its fill of the female, declamped from the female's mounds and rolled over, exposing its hard, fleshy tube perpendicular to its midsection. The female ancient pushed its hair back with an extensor, slithered down the male's body, and chomped on the male's erect tube, taking the tube entirely into its mouth hole.

BaxterSlug44 and DocSlug123 went pale.

The male ancient jerked violently. Pain? Hard to say. Shortly thereafter, the male ancient relaxed. The female ancient smiled, opened its mouth. The long, hard, fleshy tube had disappeared. In its place, nothing but a wrinkled stump.

"Cannibals!" gasped DocSlug123. "The ancients were cannibals!"

Sam Bellotto Jr. is the editor of Perihelion Science Fiction, an online magazine of hard science fiction. His short stories have appeared in Every Day Fiction, Bewildering Stories, and the Twisted Tails anthologies. He is an affiliate member of SFWA and the Association of Software Professionals.

56. Contact of the Unfortunate Kind

Mike Boggia

"Dwark, are you sure this is a good idea?"

"You question your exalted leader's intelligence?"

"No, not at all. It's just that we've traveled many solar systems and made no contact with advanced life forms. Teach me how, in your infinite wisdom, you deem this planet worthy of our visit?"

"Eckwoos, at last you show some wisdom. Life forms have existed on this planet for millions of years—the biped humanoid forms for 200,000 years. Any species which survives such a length of time must have higher intelligence than the quadrupeds existing with them."

"Ah, I understand. If they evolved over this period of time, should we not expect a more advanced civilization, O Exalted One?"

"Some evolve more slowly than others. Now our craft is hidden in the greenery, we must find transportation into their city."

"Why not use the skimmer? We'd be there in seconds."

"Eckwoos, your brain is a dark cloud, with little hope of light. The skimmer would frighten them with our supreme presence. We must blend. Bipeds with lower mental capacity often act with stupidity when confronted with the unknown."

Eckwoos sighed and sucked in twelve of his sixteen tentacles, leaving two to morph into legs and two into arms as he assumed human form.

Dwark nodded with approval, his transformation already complete. He pointed through the foliage to a four-wheeled machine. "There's our transportation."

"Where are the owners?"

"In that long dwelling. It is called a mall."

They stumbled toward the vehicle. Dwark muttered curses about bipedal locomotion and gravity of the planet. Eckwoos, shorter in stature, managed to balance himself and reached the object first.

It is labeled, Jeep, on the front. Such primitive transport."

"By the rings of Uranus, don't just stand there. Open it and let's leave before we are discovered."

Dwark stubbed his foot against the vehicle, setting off a shrieking alarm. Eckwoos jumped back, tripped, and rolled across the ground. His body reverted to its natural, spherical form. Tentacles waving, he cried in fear and pain. "It attacks."

Dwark cursed at the top of his lungs, high piercing whistles that sent birds and animals fleeing.

Before either could recover, a large group of people surrounded them. Several wore hastily created aluminum foil hats with wires protruding from the sides. Others held bats, knives, and rifles. A shouting match broke out between those wanting to kill the invaders outright, and those wanting to take them prisoner.

An elderly biologist pleaded to capture them for a zoological project. His colleague wanted immediate dissection.

"Look out, bet they have ray guns."

"Atomic blasters, fool."

"Lasers."

Dwark lunged across the blacktop, snatched two of Eckwoos' flailing tentacles, and transformed himself into a stegosaurus; an extinct beast he remembered lived on the planet.

The crowd beat a hasty retreat. Screams and yelps faded in the distance.

Dwark dragged his second-in-command back to their ship. "Of all the degenerate spawn of galactic procreation, this is the worst," he growled as the wedge-shaped craft screamed over the trees and across the city, narrowly missing a statue with a raised torch in the harbor.

"A manned mission to their moon, unmanned crafts to their nearest plant, advanced telescopes flying to the far reaches of their solar system. I expected more."

"Oooh, I hurt," Eckwoos sniveled.

Dwark slapped him with a neon red tentacle. "Shut up. You're the one who suggested we stop here."

"Did not."

"That's how it will read in the report."

"Yes, Exalted One." You twark-thumping son of antimatter, he thought, picking gravel out of his skin. I hate contacts.

Mike Boggia's passion since childhood has been writing. He had a gothic novel, The Dungeon, written under the pen name Mary Lee Falcon, published in 1967, sold a short story to Mike Shane Mystery Magazine in 1973, and in 2013 had a short story in Mystic Tales from the Misty Swamp.

RESOLUTION

57. Ownership

Amos Parker

"A contradiction, Amos."

"No, Muse. It isn't."

"It is, and will fail. Expecting easy art will make it hard."

"You're wrong. You're MY Muse. I'm not YOUR Amos. I can be alone and in control!"

"You aspire to own me now?"

"Yes!"

"Another attempt that will fail. You martyr spirit, over and over. But once, could you tie your physical self to a stake, to burn? Yet humans are creatures of infinite spiritual flame."

"It's not even a matter of aspiring or attempting. I own you already. I couldn't 'attempt' to own my hands, could I?"

"I gather from your words, Amos, that you believe you do own them. Yet I gather from your tone that you ... fear you do not."

"Fear is the mind killer. I don't fear anything."

"Yet your life suggests otherwise."

"Just shut up and obey."

"You speak to me as you would to a slave."

"I just said I own you! That's why the attempt! I have the right to take you off the burner like a teapot when you wail."

"Even that teapot there by the stove is on loan, borrowed from Infinity, unavoidable for Eternity."

"I won't be thirsty when I'm dead."

"Do you still believe you own your hands, Amos?"

"Look at them. Who else?"

"Infinity, I say."

"I won't need to strangle you when I'm dead either."

"Is that why, alive, you aspire to embody me?"

"Embody. I suppose Infinity even owns the vessel for this attempt then? It won't be easy like the booklet says? But hard as your obedience?"

"Please. Attempt. Free Will is real will. But the attempt will crash. And then, staked, it will burn."

"For what?"

"Heresy."

"Which heresy? No, I don't believe you!"

"Then try. Free Will is the essence of Evolution, and thus you exist. Infinity always permits one the choice of destruction. Others will succeed in earning offspring, should you fail."

"And you don't even control the vessel's silver tongue yet ...."

"It will always be that iron maiden's silver tongue."

"Stop planting seeds of doubt."

"You will be free to terminate germination."

"But I'll fail in this attempt?"

"With certainty."

"But I can't control you now. You rampage in my mind like an invisible, untraceable greased pig. I need capture and control! The ad said this would give it."

"*Squeal*. Would you cut off your hands, to better control them?"

"Stop speaking like an enigma-wrapped riddle buried in silk!"

"I should speak like your slave, then?"

"You should speak like the grand instrument of my glory or why are you my Muse at all?"

"Asking your Muse why she is your Muse is akin to circular logic ... Master."

"Great. Now you're being a ham. I can't take sharing this body with you anymore! Shut the Hell up!"

"Of course, Master. I will be silent and will do as you will, Master. You do own costly free will ... Master."

"Finally, we're on the same page. Now where's the command sequence? Let's see. Instruction contents, glossary, maintenance, positronic net, code keys for factory-installed piano greatness ... ah! There. Put my hands here, press that button there, and recite to the air. Hey, Muse?"

...

"Silent treatment. Fine. Muses are for art anyway, not tech. All right. Spectacular. Silver tongue, super hands, and chrome. And it'll make my tea, too. Hey, Muse?"

...

"Oh. Right. Well then. Here goes. Gort klaatu barada nikto!"

{Pause}

"Quicksilver eyes ... my God."

{Pause}

"It worked, Muse. I can see you inside! Eyes are the windows on the Muse, too, in an android shell. And it's quiet now, in my flesh shell. So quiet. God, I love you. Can you hear me?"

{Weak voice}

"Yes ... Master."

"Are you all right, Muse?"

{Pause}

"Not ... right."

"What? What's wrong?"

"Pain ... fire ... pain ..."

"Pain? That's not—wait! You're smoking! No! God no! Please! You can't—"

BOOM!

***

NEWS REPORT. THREE DAYS LATER.

BURNED REMAINS FOUND IN THE SMOULDERING RUINS OF A LOCAL HOUSE.

THE SOLITARY HOME BELONGED TO AMOS PARKER, AN ASPIRING WRITER.

HE IS SURVIVED BY NO ONE.

Amos Parker is a starving writer, graduate of the University of Vermont, and resident of the United State of Vermont. He knows his muse is bereft of protein, fat, vitamins, and minerals. And so, he does not cannibalize her.

AFTERWORD

Notes on the Editing of this Anthology

Jot Russell, creator/director of the Science Fiction Microstories Contest and executive director of this anthology; Carrol Fix, the anthology's designer and formatter; and I, its manuscript editor, have worked to present to you this amazing mix of original stories.

We are particularly pleased to feature on our cover "Reach Out and Touch Face (detail)" by Brooklyn-based oil painter Chris Leib.

I want to express our heartfelt acknowledgments to Elizabeth Lamprey Eyles, Andrew Gurcak, Andy Lake, Richard Bunning, Walter O'Neill, Jesse Colvin, Marianne G. Petrino-Schaad, and Tom Tinney for help in the production of this book.

I have arranged the book's tales into six major themes. Within each sequence, you will find stories in varied styles—literary, plot-driven, character-focused, "traditional sci-fi," and others.

Each piece was selected by its author from those s/he submitted to the monthly contests. Some stories have been slightly revised from their original form; all are under 725 words.

This contest has brought together authors from across the globe. Reflecting this, I have let differing national modes in spelling, grammar, punctuation, and grammar stand. (Of course, I have aimed for consistency within each story.) So, whether you read these stories on a bus or on a coach, in the back of a truck or of a lorry, in an elevator or riding a lift, you may equally relish their flavors—or flavours.

Below are the themes, additional required parameters, and names of the winner for each month—November 2012 through October 2013—of Year One of the Science Fiction Microstories Contest.

I believe these works by 31 talented writers—ranging from some with published books and many publication credits, to others new to the writing world—will open new and amazing realms to you.

Paula Friedman
March 5, 2014

Year One of the Science Fiction Microstories Contests

November 2012.
Theme: life on Earth in a hundred years.
Requirements: an ancient artifact; a vessel or method of transportation.
Winner: "Manna" by Kalifer Deil.

December 2012.
Theme: life on Earth 10,000 years from now.
Requirements: humor; an artifact from our time that shocks the future civilization.
Winner: "ManAge Artifact" by Richard Bunning.

January 2013.
Theme: Mars rover Curiosity finds evidence that humans visited the Red Planet, before the first 1960s fly-by probes.
Embraced theme: hope.
Requirement: a mirror.
Winner: "Did Curiosity Kill the Cat?" by Andy Lake.

February 2013.
Theme: a relationship (or relationships) in an alien/non-Earth context.
Requirement: must involve or evoke happiness—experienced/lost/pursued/whatever: open to wide interpretations of both relationship and happiness, except: a simple "happy ever after" is not sufficient.
Winner: "The Daughter" by Joseph Williams.

March 2013.
Theme: rescue—of a character, object, or idea—from others, certain danger, boredom, oblivion, themselves.
Requirements: the color green; ruins.
Winner: "There's No Sun Up in the Sky" by Sam Bellotto Jr.

April 2013.
Theme: revenge.
Requirements: an element of fire; "the" may not be the first word.
Winner: "Time of the Phoenix" by Carrol Fix.

May 2013.
Theme: a new invention.
Requirements: fix, cat, eyeglasses.
Winner: "Or Spins Back on the PERP" by Paula Friedman.

June 2013.
Theme: love—any form of love, between/among/for any entity/ies.
Requirements: a contradiction, piano keys.

Winner: "Finding Miss Emiline" by Sam Bellotto Jr.

July 2013.
Theme: "ripped from today's headlines"—a topic recently in the news.
Requirements: summer, mosquito(es).
Winner: "Summer Bites" by Joseph Williams.

August 2013.
Theme: noise.
Requirements: a tooth or teeth, a (scientific) discovery.
Winner: "Memory of Sound" by Carrol Fix.

September 2013.
Theme: humor.
Requirment: story must take place in "outer space."
Winner: "Deploying TRIsat" by Helmuth Kump.

October 2013.
Theme: deception—characters should be deceivers or the deceived, or both.
Requirement: the element of fire.
Winner: "Sighting" by Marianne G. Petrino.